Seduction at the Chateau

Bleu Blanc Rogue
Book 1

Delphine Roy

Dragonblade Publishing, Inc. is an imprint of Kathryn Le Veque Novels, Inc.
P.O. Box 23
Moreno Valley, CA 92556
ceo@dragonbladepublishing.com

Produced in the United States of America

First Edition January 2024
Trade Paperback Edition

ARE YOU SIGNED UP FOR DRAGONBLADE'S BLOG?

You'll get the latest news and information on exclusive giveaways, exclusive excerpts, coming releases, sales, free books, cover reveals and more.

Check out our complete list of authors, too!

No spam, no junk. That's a promise!

Sign Up Here

www.dragonbladepublishing.com

Dearest Reader;

Thank you for your support of a small press. At Dragonblade Publishing, we strive to bring you the highest quality Historical Romance from some of the best authors in the business. Without your support, there is no 'us', so we sincerely hope you adore these stories and find some new favorite authors along the way.

Happy Reading!

CEO, Dragonblade Publishing

Chapter One

Paris, May 1801

"WELL, DO YOU see her?"

Guy de Cazal stretched his neck, his gaze flitting through the crowd of revelers illuminated by the golden light of the lanterns. They went to and fro, in colorful frocks and coats, raucous laughter erupting over the lively music playing on a nearby platform. It seemed as though all of Paris had come to the Tivoli Garden to enjoy the first warm evening of the season—surely *she* would be there.

"Not yet," Guy told his companion, Nicolas Lefevre. "Keep an eye out, will you?"

"If she comes accompanied by Xavier de Brienne, we'll spot her easily enough. That fop is a head taller than everyone."

Guy snorted. *Fop* was too kind a word for that arrogant imbecile. He readjusted his royal blue velvet jacket over his fitted waistcoat, briefly checking if his sable hair was suitably coiffed. "Height does not a man make."

Nicolas gave a little laugh. "Don't worry, old fellow, you are perfectly *à la mode*. The ladies around us have been giving you the eye since we got here."

"Maybe they're looking at your splendid attire," Guy replied.

With his taste for colorful stripes and a fringe of blond curls falling over his forehead, Nicolas embodied the more extravagant fashion that was all the rage among the smart set. Guy favored more subdued clothes himself, but still, it would not do if he were anything other than striking tonight. In spite of his jest, he took assurance in his friend's words and glanced discreetly around him; indeed, among the ladies present, their shawls slouching to reveal shockingly thin muslin dresses, many were slipping him flirtatious glances. But he only had eyes for one.

"Ah, here she is," Nicolas said with a nudge. "Right behind you."

Guy looked over his shoulder. Victoire Le Plessis Tailland sauntered past the revelers. With her golden curls framing her flawless face, she was a vision in a pure white dress, draped like a toga over her shapely figure and cut scandalously low, as if to nip in the bud any suggestion that she might be an innocent debutante... But why did such a vision have to turn up on the arm of a haughty-faced bastard?

"Madame Le Plessis," Guy greeted her with a gallant bow of his head. "Monsieur de Brienne. Quite a party, is it not?"

"Monsieur de Cazal, Monsieur Lefevre," De Brienne replied, looking down at them from his long, slightly crooked nose. "I wasn't expecting such a crowd, but then that's what happens when you stray from the more exclusive venues of the capital."

"By God, man, don't you believe in democracy in this day and age?" Nicolas taunted him.

"I fail to find your humor to my taste, *monsieur*," De Brienne sniffed.

"Xavier, behave," Victoire commanded, giving his arm a playful slap with her fan. "I happen to find the Tivoli Gardens delightful. Listen, they're playing a waltz."

"Might I persuade you to grant me the favor of a dance, *madame*?" Guy asked Victoire.

Victoire watched him for a moment, her dark eyes glittering with mischief, then she turned to Xavier with a charming pout.

"You don't mind, do you, Xavier? It would be inexcusable of me to turn down such a polite offer."

De Brienne was trapped. Guy bit back a triumphant smirk. Victoire wasn't looking to replace her husband with a possessive lover, and De Brienne couldn't very well ask her to refuse without coming off as a clinging buffoon.

"As you wish, my angel." He took her hand and kissed it. "I shall wait for you here."

"I'll do my best not to keep her," Guy said with cheeky grin.

De Brienne looked as if he had bitten a lemon in half. That in itself was almost as sweet as having Victoire sashay over to him and slip her arm in his. As they were making their way toward the dancing area, Guy let his eyes roam over her enticing cleavage.

"You look positively delectable tonight," he murmured. "It's a wonder every man present isn't fighting for your favor."

"You do flatter me so, Guy," she replied. "I see you wore my favorite jacket, the one that matches your eyes. We make a handsome pair, don't we?"

They reached the dancing area and he swept her in his arms, spinning her around in time with the heady rhythm of the waltz. Victoire kept up with him, her step graceful and light, her expression one of elegant self-confidence. A trail of stares and whispers followed them as they passed. Victoire was quickly rising as one of the great beauties of Paris, known for her luxurious tastes and her revealing attire, and with her at his arm, Guy would gain entry into the best salons in the capital and the wealth of pleasures they had to offer.

He was dizzy and breathless—from the waltz, from the buoyant music and glimmering lights, from the thrilling possibilities that lay before him. Gone were the days of feeling like he was stuck in an endless tunnel of despair, exiled in a foreign country, nearly destitute, watching helplessly as his mother drowned in her own sorrow. Tonight, the world was his. *Theirs.*

The waltz ended but Guy still held Victoire, a captive of the expensive and exotic scent wafting from her skin. He leaned to whisper in her ear. "Come away with me for a moment."

"Not too long, or I'm afraid Xavier will get into his head to challenge you to a duel."

Guy shook his head. "I don't know what you see in that imbecile."

"He's almost as generous as my husband, and it wouldn't be fair to burden only one man with my gambling debts," Victoire retorted with a crystalline laugh.

Guy tugged playfully on her hand and led her away from the dancing area, in the opposite direction from which they had come. Tall hedgerows lined winding paths, a convenient place for an intimate meeting. So intimate, in fact, that Guy thought he could hear the squeals and grunts of a couple fornicating not far from them.

Victoire raised an eyebrow. "Why, Monsieur de Cazal, do you mean to ravish me?"

"Only if you're willing." Guy stopped and turned toward her, snaking an arm around her thin waist. "You know I have been longing for this moment."

Victoire resisted his embrace ever so slightly but didn't push him away. "Very well, then. Make your case."

"Your eyes and lips haunt my dreams, *madame*, and my ardor for you knows no bounds."

"Go on," she purred sensually.

Damnation, she was exquisite. The way she teased and toyed with him promised the most exhilarating bedsport of his life. One night with her would feel like reaching the peak of the Mont Blanc.

"I know I'm not as wealthy as De Brienne, but if you were to take me as a lover, I would worship you, body and soul, like the Athenians bowing before the wise and fearsome Minerva. I would never let a single one of your desires go unsatisfied."

"That sounds promising." She let him brush his lips against hers only for a moment before untangling herself from his embrace. "But you see, I am not one to share the attention of any man with another woman."

What was she talking about? Guy was trying to keep his tone even in spite of her rebuff. "There is no other woman. No one but you, my goddess. You are incomparable."

"Really? Are you not engaged to Antonia Saint Yves?"

Her words landed on him like a block of pavement to the head. "I… Who told you that?"

"Marie-Louise, of course. She met the Saint Yves family while they were all exiled in London."

Guy bit back a curse. In a world of busybodies with nothing better to do than wag their tongues all day, Marie-Louise Aubertin was the worst.

"It was an agreement concluded between our parents a decade ago, before we were forced to leave France," he explained. "But all of them have since passed, and I haven't seen Antonia in years."

"Still, one never knows what promise was made in spirit to your parents before they died. Tragedy makes some people sentimental."

Dark, roiling anger reared its ugly head, but he tamped it down as quickly as it rose. No. No more. He wouldn't let it overtake him again.

"No such promise exists," he said coolly. "Are we not at the dawn of a new era, where parents no longer decide whom their children must marry, and women are free to choose whom they love?"

"I'm glad to hear you say it. Though I must tell you right now, I won't divorce my husband. What would I get out of it that I don't already have? The dear is perfectly content staying in the countryside while I'm in the city and providing for my expenses. Plus he's in no state to get me with child and ruin my figure. It's ideal, really."

Of course it was. All of Parisian society knew that Monsieur Le Plessis Tailland was bedridden with the gout most of the time, and that he'd always shown more interest for hunting pheasants and breeding dogs than for his lovely young wife.

He reached for her hand again, pulling her back to him. "Nothing, then, stands in the way of our passion."

"Not so fast," Victoire said, fanning herself with maddening aloofness. "There is no lack of gentlemen offering me such opportunities. If I were to truly give myself to you, I must make sure I'm betting on the right horse."

"If you're referring to stamina, I guarantee you I am unequaled," he rumbled seductively. "But since I cannot prove it to you in the bedroom, how shall I proceed?"

She gave him an impish smile. "What do you say we make a little game of it? In a few weeks, there's to be a party at the Aubertin's country chateau. Why don't I get Marie-Louise to invite Antonia?"

Guy's instincts sounded a sharp alarm, but he smothered them immediately. Nothing would stop him from making Victoire his own. "I'm listening."

"If you can seduce her during our stay, then cast her off, that will prove to me beyond the shadow of a doubt that you hold no attachment to the past, but also that your prowess as a lover is unsurpassed."

This gave him pause. True, he hadn't seen Antonia for a very long time, and even though their respective fathers had been the closest of friends, he barely knew her. He was six years her senior, and back when they all lived in Chartres, he had little interest in a spotty, awkward girl who blushed every time he opened his mouth. Still, what Victoire was asking would undoubtedly have serious consequences, not least because Antonia's older brother Jerome might decide to put a lead ball through his head. Thankfully, last Guy had heard, Jerome was still in London, training to be an architect like his father.

"This will gravely harm her reputation if word gets out," he stated.

Victoire shrugged her creamy shoulders. "She'll simply go back to her provincial backwoods and none will be the wiser.

Besides, did you not just say women should be free to love whom they choose? You're not a brute, Guy, you're not going to force yourself on the girl. If you are apt at the art of seduction, she'll come to you readily."

"Antonia is… different. She's the youngest of her siblings, and she's always been sheltered and protected."

"All the better, then. She'll get an education out of it." Victoire's dark eyes suddenly turned hard and glinted with the shine of rare onyx. "It's a lesson all women must learn, sooner or later."

IN THE AFTERNOONS, the drawing room in the Saint Yves family home was always filled with the exuberant noises of playful children and their parents' admonishments, but today, Antonia heard none of it. Her fingers trembled slightly as she reread the letter she had received that morning for what seemed like the hundredth time.

It would be a pleasure and a delight to have you join us at Verneuil, as I so very much enjoyed your company when these most tragic circumstances brought us together in England. I daresay that a particular gentleman will be most happy to see you again after such a long time apart. Since you were unhappily separated in spite of your promise to each other, I am glad if I can be of service in allowing you to rekindle your connection…

Antonia folded the letter back up and stared absently out the window. In the distance, beyond the courtyard of the Saint Yves domain, she could see the gray slate roofs and the twin steeples of the Chartres cathedral. It was a familiar landscape, one she had grown up with, one she had dreamed of during the long years of exile, yet today it brought her no comfort.

"Toinette, dear, is something the matter?"

She turned to see her sister Honorine looking at her with a frown. Antonia handed her the letter.

"It's an invitation from Marie-Louise and François Aubertin," she said. "You remember them, don't you?"

Honorine nodded. "The Aubertins, yes. Those charming people we met in London. I particularly recall her being quite the entertainer. I do not believe I've heard anyone gossip with such unabashed relish."

"Well, Madame Aubertin bids me to stay at the Château de Verneuil, a month from now."

"How kind," Honorine replied, then scooped up her youngest child, a boy of two who was tugging at her skirt, to settle him on her hip while she read. "*A particular gentleman. Does she mean...?*"

"Guy de Cazal. Yes. It can only be him."

Though Antonia forced her face into a mask of indifference, her heart was hammering against her chest. She remembered precisely when she'd told Madame Aubertin of her connection to Guy. It had been a cold, rainy evening in London, during a cold, rainy winter, when there was nothing else to do but play cards, drink punch, and share news of France. By supper time, their hostess had been passably tipsy and had asked Antonia if she had a sweetheart waiting for her back in the motherland, and Antonia had been silly enough to tell her that Guy de Cazal was her intended, as it had been their parents' sincerest wish for them to marry.

What had she been thinking? At the time, it had seemed perfectly harmless. It was hard to believe that they would ever be able to return to France, harder still to imagine she would see Guy again. Their lives had been ripped apart so brutally when they'd fled the Terror that nothing was certain anymore.

And yet here she was, standing in the same drawing room where she had spent so many hours as a child, watching Honorine's children play on the same faded rugs. There was no nursery in the Saint Yves home; their parents had considered themselves as forward-thinking and enlightened, and spending as much time as possible with their children was part of the progressive ideas they had put into place. They would be proud to see Honorine and her husband Stanislas carrying on their legacy.

As for Antonia, her parents had asked only one thing of her: to marry Guy. A promise she thought she would never have to keep… until she read that blasted letter. A letter confirming what they'd heard upon returning to Chartres: that Guy was alive and staying in Paris, though both of his parents were deceased.

"I never thought that this would come back to haunt me," she said dejectedly. "When I told Madame Aubertin about Guy, she had already drunk five glasses of punch."

"Do you think Guy is planning on making your engagement official?" Honorine asked.

"Why on earth would he do that? We haven't seen each other in a decade. Besides, if that were the case, wouldn't he have written to me himself? It was only by chance we found out he wasn't still in exile, or dead. If Stanislas hadn't met Monsieur Fournier in the street…"

Lazare Fournier had been the right hand of Guy's father, and together they had run the most successful banking business in Chartres. He was the one who had told Stanislas that Guy needed to stay in Paris for the time being, as he was wrestling with the government to retrieve the family assets that had been stolen during the Revolution.

"Perhaps Guy prefers discussing these matters with you in person," Honorine suggested.

Which wasn't doing her a favor. Antonia would rather be rejected and humiliated with a curt missive she could burn in the fireplace than having to face Guy and ridicule herself. She'd put all of that behind her—or at least she thought she had. Apparently traveling across the Channel and back wasn't enough to put a definite end to past mistakes.

"Be that as it may, I'm not going," Antonia said, snatching back the letter and crumpling it in her fist. "I'll have to send Madame Aubertin my regrets."

Honorine set her son down and he ran back to play with his five siblings.

"Jeanne," she called out to the eldest, a nine-year old girl who had the same glossy russet hair and gray eyes as her mother and her aunt. "I need to talk with Toinette in private. Can you look after the little ones, my sweet? We'll be right outside the door if you need us."

Antonia reluctantly followed Honorine out into the corridor. Her sister gave a deep sigh and held out her hand until Antonia relented and gave her the crumpled letter.

"You are free to heed my advice or not," Honorine said, "but I think you should go. You are four and twenty, dearest, and it's high time you went back out into society. A young unmarried woman such as yourself shouldn't spend her days helping me around the house or building block castles with the children. We all love you dearly, but it is unfair to ask you to stay here and ruin your chances to one day have a family of your own."

"You're not asking me anything," Antonia muttered. "I stay here because I choose to."

Which wasn't a lie, but it wasn't the entire truth either. How many nights had she laid awake in bed, staring at the ceiling, wondering when her turn would come to leave the nest? Plagued by thoughts of fading away into the background as a spinster, her capacity to envision a future for herself crippled with every year that passed?

But she could not confide in her sister. They had only just returned to a semblance of normalcy a few months ago, and the last thing Honorine and Stanislas needed was her complaining about the monotony of her days.

Honorine frowned. "Jerome and I were perhaps too protective of you. After Mother and Father were taken from us by that terrible fever, after we were forced into exile…" Tears sprang to her eyes but she quickly brushed them away. "It was such a dreadful time. We were all clinging to each other, weren't we? But the Revolution is over now. And you deserve to experience a bit of freedom and merriment. If Jerome were here, he would say the same."

Antonia raised an eyebrow. The words *freedom* and *merriment* had never crossed the lips of their hard-nosed brother. "Really?"

"All right, maybe not," Honorine admitted. "But he does want to see you make a good match."

And Guy de Cazal was undeniably a good match. He was the only heir of his father's business, and slowly but surely, all the property and wealth that had been confiscated during the Reign of Terror was being returned. If Guy was successful in getting it back, he would be in possession of a small fortune.

Not only that, but unless some tragic accident or disease had radically altered his appearance, he was also the most handsome man Antonia had ever met.

She could easily picture his tall, broad frame, his easy smile, his hair such a dark shade of brown it appeared to be almost black until a ray of sun revealed its warm, rich color. And his eyes—oh, those deep blue eyes, how they had made her adolescent heart flutter. To her, Guy had been the paragon of masculinity: there was no horse too wild for him to ride, no discussion he shied away from, no challenge he didn't want to undertake. And foolish dreamer that she was, she had actually thought he might wake up one day and take an interest in her.

It had only taken one cruel twist of fate to find out that this would never happen. Antonia remembered it as her first stinging slap of reality, before the rest of their world collapsed around them.

She shook her head. The past was the past, and she needed to focus on the situation at hand. "What if I want to stay here with you?"

"This will always be your home, Toinette," Honorine replied warmly. "But I see the books you read, whenever you have a spare moment. Can you tell me in all honesty that there isn't a part of you who wishes to see more of the world?"

True, immersing herself in tales of travel and adventure and romance was Antonia's favorite pastime, but it was one thing to read about them and quite another to live them. After their long exile, part of her recoiled at the idea of stepping foot outside the house.

The other part, however, swelled with an irrepressible desire for *more*.

"Look at it this way," Honorine pressed on. "Regardless of Guy's intentions and your opinion of him, this might be a chance to meet other eligible gentlemen. The Aubertins are wealthy and well-connected. A stay at their place will give you the same advantages as a season in the capital, at far less of an expense for us."

When it came to family matters, more often than not, her sister's practical side prevailed. Antonia could sense she was running out of arguments. Objectively, this was an opportunity a young woman of her station couldn't afford to refuse. And should she never marry, she would be a financial burden to her siblings until the end of her days. Honorine and Stanislas had never once complained about this, but it wasn't fair to simply assume they would take care of her when they already had six children to raise.

"Who would go with me?" she asked, grasping for straws. "I cannot possibly make the trip unchaperoned."

Honorine smoothed over the letter. "It says here that a certain Madame Rouget, a most respectable widow, would be willing to chaperone you during your stay. As for the trip, it's only a day and a half by carriage. You can take Lisette with you and she'll act as your chambermaid."

"How will you manage without her? Who will help you dress and do your hair?"

"I'll hire a girl from the village. In any case, it's high time I start making inquiries to employ more help, now that little Baptiste can walk." She sighed. "Jeanne alone cannot help me when they're all intent of wreaking havoc."

As if on cue, a loud clatter came from the drawing room, followed by a stern reproach from Jeanne and a high-pitched wail. Honorine gathered her skirts and ran back inside, and Antonia was left with the thought that going to Verneuil might be just trading one type of chaos for another.

Chapter Two

THE HORSE'S HOOVES thundered up the trail. His muscles tense, his gaze alert, Guy pushed his mount as fast as it could go, and soon they were galloping at full speed towards the Château de Verneuil. It lay on top of a grassy slope, in the middle of a sprawling domain of scattered woods, winding country paths and stone follies. On the other side of the chateau, which had been extended from a hunting lodge into a full-fledged neoclassical beauty, there was a meticulously tended garden *à la française* built around a large fountain.

It was the perfect place to spend stifling summer days far from the city… and even more so in charming company. Guy slowed his exhausted horse and let him recuperate by grazing on the lush grass. He was breathless himself, but nowhere near as tired as he'd like to be; the fire coursing through his veins had only been excited by the ride. In the last few weeks, he'd abstained from his usual pleasure seeking, knowing fully well that his seduction skills were sharper when the need was more acute. He'd even foregone solitary release, something he had never even considered before, and as a result, an energy unlike any he'd known before was humming right under the surface of his skin.

But it would all be worth it if he could channel it into his enticement of Antonia, who had accepted Madame Aubertin's invitation and was due to arrive any day.

Guy absently patted his horse's neck and glanced behind him at Nicolas, who was trotting over. It should be simple enough to get this over with quickly; how difficult could it be to tempt a naive, inexperienced woman into a romantic encounter? One thing he clearly remembered about Toinette, as her family called her, was that she always had her nose stuck in a book, reading Rousseau or Richardson, filling her mind with sentimental ideals.

All he had to do was crush the niggling feeling of guilt that arose when he thought of taking advantage of her in this way.

Nicolas finally reached him and halted as well. "Good grief, man, you took off like a cannonball. I would have broken my neck trying to follow you."

Guy shrugged. "Felt like a bit of a thrill."

His friend took a handkerchief from his pocket and wiped his sweaty brow. "You had better be efficient in bedding that *demoiselle*. I'll not have you risking your life because you've deprived yourself of your usual exertions."

"Don't you worry about that. I shall be as precise and deadly as the point of a saber."

"Or swing it around recklessly, hoping it'll meet its mark."

They both laughed and started walking their horses back to the stables. Once the animals had been left in the care of the stable hands, they made their way back to the chateau. Some of the guests were sitting on the terrace under a gazebo, enjoying refreshments; among them was Victoire, who looked splendid in a pale yellow frock that frothed around her like a haze of sunshine. When she spotted Guy, she granted him a dazzling smile. De Brienne, who was sitting next to her, scowled.

"Oh, Monsieur de Cazal, Monsieur Lefevre, won't you join us?"

A buxom matron dressed in a pink dress, her brown hair done in tight curls and peppered with flowers, waved them over the table where she was sitting with Marie-Louise Aubertin. Claudine Rouget was Marie-Louise's dearest friend, and the two of them spent all hours of the day and evening chattering and drinking claret.

"Madame Rouget, Madame Aubertin," Guy said gallantly. "How are you faring in this heat?"

"I have been just telling Marie-Louise that she has devised the most thrilling guest list for this little holiday," Claudine tittered. Her rather opulent chest, squeezed into tight stays, wobbled almost up to her neck. "Oh, I can imagine the sort of mischief two young bucks such as yourself will get up to."

"I assure you, *madame*, our intentions are entirely honorable," Nicolas said. "At least mine are."

"Well, we'll just have to see about that. This scorching weather slows the mind but heats up the blood, does it not?"

Guy raised an eyebrow at his friend who bit back a chuckle. Nicolas had never had an honorable intention in his life, but something told Guy the two women were experienced enough not to be fooled by any pretense of good behavior.

"Do sit down, *messieurs*," Marie-Louise said. "You must be parched!"

"Thank you, *madame*, but I'm desperate for a change of clothes," Guy said.

Nicolas sat down in an empty chair and smoothed his hands over his saffron riding coat. Leave it to him to look like a fashion plate after a ride in this weather. Even his damn cravat was still knotted to perfection. "You go on," he told Guy. "I think I'll have a drink or two before retiring."

"Oh, please do, Monsieur Lefevre!" Claudine said, clapping her hands in delight. "You can tell us how you got that scar on your brow. It makes you look like a devilish pirate!"

"It's actually quite a tale…" Nicolas started.

"I'll leave you to it," Guy said with a nod.

He went inside, a smile playing on his lips. Claudine Rouget's raucous behavior may have been considered unseemly in more conservative circles, but it suited him just fine. She was supposed to act as Antonia's chaperone during her stay, and there would be no difficulty in escaping her vigilance, which by evening was solely focused on her wine glass.

As he made his way toward the grand staircase, Guy whipped off his jacket and hat and loosened his cravat. He had always been a man to enjoy a challenge. If this was too easy, he might get bored with it before he even began.

His thoughts froze in time with his steps. The *majordome* stood at the open door and a new guest had just entered the front hall.

Antonia.

Guy stared at her, stunned. He had immediately recognized her, and yet the lovely creature standing in front of him in a dark blue traveling outfit was nothing like what he remembered. Delicate feminine features, a shapely body, flawless skin... His rational mind had known he would be facing a young woman of twenty-four and not an adolescent of fourteen, but the contrast between the two images hit him like a punch to the gut.

When she saw him, she let out a little gasp but quickly regained her bearing.

"Toinette," he blurted out, then remembered his manners and bowed his head. "I... I am pleased to see you after such a long time apart."

She dropped into a stiff curtsy. "Monsieur de Cazal."

So formal. So frosty. What a fool he was, bandying about her nickname like a blasted schoolboy. A hot flush rose to his face.

"Did you have an agreeable trip?" he asked, trying for a polite smile. If she could hide behind a façade of manners, so could he.

"Quite."

"And your family? Are they well?"

She took off her bonnet, revealing a messy bundle of reddish curls, and fiddled with the ribbons. "Jerome has stayed behind in London to finish his apprenticeship. Honorine, Stanislas and the children are in Chartres. Stanislas has taken over our father's cabinet."

"How many children do they have now?"

"Six."

"My, that is impressive. Would that everyone was so efficient at producing citizens for the Republic!"

Antonia stared at him blankly. Damn it all. That kind of sarcastic quip would have earned him some laughs in an elegant salon, but he should have known better than to try it on her. What the hell was the matter with him? He raked a hand through his hair and suddenly remembered his disheveled attire.

"You'll have to excuse me, I was just out riding."

"You're excused, *monsieur*. I was about to go up to my room and settle in."

"Of course. Would you care to join me on the terrace afterwards?"

She lifted her chin. Guy was dumbfounded. Since when did little Toinette *lift her chin* at anyone? Well, she wasn't little anymore. Her perfectly rounded breasts and slim waist were proof enough of that. Though her face was equally enchanting: a long, straight nose, heavy-lidded gray eyes, rosebud lips... How had he never noticed before?

"Please don't feel the need to extend such courtesies to me on behalf of our previous acquaintance," she replied. "I am certain you have better things to do with your time."

And with that, she turned away and started up the stairs before he could say another word.

Guy stared after her. What the devil had just happened? Antonia's cold demeanor didn't make any sense. What could he have possibly done to deserve such a rebuff when they hadn't seen each other in years? He would have to figure it out, press her for more, discern what grudge was lurking in her mind. Getting to her would be far more difficult than he had anticipated.

And if there was one thing that got his blood pumping, it was a challenge.

ANTONIA LOOKED OUT the window to the vast expanse of greenery that surrounded the chateau. She felt a little better now that she had changed out of her traveling clothes and washed, but as soon as Lisette had left her alone to go settle in the servants' quarters, all the details of her unexpected encounter with Guy came flooding back into her mind.

He was just as handsome as she remembered. No, handsomer still. At twenty, Guy had been a bright-eyed young man with a devilish grin and an air of confidence that lit up any room. At thirty, his body was leaner, his face drawn by adversity, his expression harder in spite of his unfailing politeness. Yet all of it only made his blue eyes more startling and his presence more powerful. Ten years ago, she had been utterly charmed by him. Now, she was unnerved, which was worse, especially since their discussion had lasted all but a minute.

Antonia looked to the horizon, trying to picture the length of the road that separated her from her family, cutting through the burnt gold of the fields basking under the summer sun. Too long. At that moment, all she wanted to do was pack up again and go back in the other direction.

Her sister's face appeared in her mind, benevolent but stern. What would she say if she were here? *You've stood your ground. You made him understand that you were no longer the lovesick little girl you once were, and if he wants to obtain your friendship, he will have to work for it. It was well done, Toinette!*

Yes, Honorine would be proud. And if her sister believed she could prevail, Antonia needed to believe it herself.

Her spirits bolstered, she glanced down at the guests who were promenading around the centerpiece of the garden, a fountain with a large, circular pond. Almost immediately, she spotted Guy, who was walking arm in arm on the far side of the pond with a woman dressed in a pale-yellow frock and carrying an ornate parasol.

Antonia's stomach plummeted. Guy never took his eyes off his companion, engrossed in their conversation. How could he not be, when she carried herself with such elegance and poise? Suddenly, the woman halted and pivoted so that her parasol shielded her from the rest of the guests. Guy bent down towards her, and for a second they were both hidden from sight.

Long enough for a kiss.

Antonia turned away from the window, her chest painfully constricted. If she had any lingering doubt that Guy had no intention of reconnecting with her or formalizing their betrothal, they were now gone.

She sat at the dressing table and tried to put some order in her messy curls. The room she was staying in was decorated with refined taste, the walls covered in pale blue wallpaper and the furniture slightly old-fashioned, with graceful lines and floral inlays, like something out of a sentimental novel from the past century. Simply being here, surrounded by nature, ensconced in luxury, would make anyone dream of love.

She gathered her resolve. Even if Guy was as indifferent to her as he had always been, this didn't mean that she was going to cower away like some wounded animal. No, she had been invited here in her own right, and she intended to make the most of it.

With the sun slowly softening into a rosy glow, the guests were returning inside to prepare for the evening's entertainment. Lisette returned to the room, looking more excited than Antonia was.

"Never saw such haughty maids in all my days," she told Antonia as she helped her take off her plain linen frock, leaving her in her chemise and stays. "Just because they're at the service of those Parisian coquettes, they fling around the names of famous modistes and compare the lengths of silk that were used up for their mistresses' wardrobes until they run out of breath."

Antonia glanced at the dress of mauve gauze Lisette had laid out. It was one of three Honorine had insisted on having made for her trip, though they could barely afford it. Back in Chartres, it had seemed like a dress fit for a princess, more luxurious than anything Antonia had ever worn; now, she wasn't so sure.

"Don't you worry, *mademoiselle*," Lisette smiled, sensing her nervousness. "I'll bet you a gold franc that none of them have so rosy a complexion as yours, nor so fine a figure. All the silk and powder in the world can't change that."

Antonia smiled back. "It's kind of you to say so, but I'm afraid Parisians don't see it that way."

"Maybe so. But a true gentleman, one of noble stock, will perceive true beauty and distinction."

To her dismay, Antonia blushed. Was Lisette talking about Guy? Surely the servants knew what was afoot. There were no secrets in the Saint Yves household. However, Lisette fell silent and concentrated on dressing her and arranging her hair. As a finishing touch, she slid a choker of freshwater pearls around Antonia's neck—the only piece of jewelry she had kept from her late mother. All the other jewels had been sold off, one by one, while they were in London, though Honorine had managed to hold on to their mother's engagement ring.

Seeing the pearls gleaming softly around her neck made a tremor pass through Antonia's heart. She was older now than her mother when she'd married. She needed to make this stay a success, if only for her family's sake.

"There, all done," Lisette said with a satisfied smile. "You are sure to make an impression tonight, *mademoiselle*."

With her fan in hand and matching stole draped around her shoulders, Antonia took a deep breath and made her way downstairs. *Don't falter*, she told herself. *Don't look at* him. *Concentrate on greeting your hosts and introducing yourself to Madame Rouget.*

When she arrived in the parlor, there were already a dozen guests present. Thankfully, Guy was not among them. She glanced around and finally spotted Marie-Louise Aubertin.

"My dear girl!" the woman exclaimed. "How wonderful to see you! Why, you are even lovelier than you were back in London. I am so sorry I wasn't there to greet you when you arrived but when the *majordome* told me, you had already gone up to your room! Come, come, Claudine has been dying to make your acquaintance."

She said all of this practically in one breath and Antonia followed her, slightly dazed. "I thank you again for extending such a kind invitation to me, *madame*."

"Please, call me by my given name. François and I try to make things as informal as possible when we are at Verneuil. Normal society rules need not apply, at least not all of them," she added with a wink.

Before Antonia could reply, she was led in front of a curvaceous woman in a puce gown with a low neckline, sporting an extravagant plume in her brown hair. She seemed to be around forty, a few years younger than Marie-Louise, but her plump cheeks and jolly expression made it difficult to pinpoint her age.

"Claudine, I'd like you to meet Antonia Saint Yves," Marie-Louise said.

Antonia curtsied. "A pleasure, Madame Rouget."

The woman gasped. "*Seigneur*! Aren't you a pretty young thing! Fresh and delicate as a rose in bloom! But, my dear, let us not embarrass ourselves with formalities. I insist you address me as Claudine, and I shall call you Antonia."

For half a moment, words failed her. When she'd pictured having a respectable widow to chaperone her, this definitely wasn't what she had in mind.

"Would you like some vermouth? You know, the Italians drink it before dinner to whet their appetite. They call it *aperitivo*. A delightful practice, is it not?"

Not wanting to come off as impolite, Antonia opted for a safer drink. She certainly could use something to take the edge off her nerves. "Maybe a glass of claret?"

"I will see to it," Marie-Louise said, and left them.

At that moment, a beautiful young woman with blonde curls, dressed in a flowing pale blue Grecian gown, entered the room at the arm of a tall gentleman with a crooked nose. Antonia recognized her immediately, though she'd only seen her from afar a few hours earlier. She was the one who had been walking with Guy around the pond, and she was even more striking up close, with her dark eyes and aloof smile.

"Ah, I see you've spotted Victoire Le Plessis Tailland," Claudine said.

"And her husband, I suppose?" Antonia asked with foolish hope.

Claudine lowered her voice. "Oh no, that is Xavier de Brienne. Victoire's husband, Monsieur Le Plessis, hasn't been seen in society in years, but she never lacks for male companionship."

Victoire. A fitting name for such a bold woman, who thought nothing of showing herself in public with her lover. Antonia knew that this wasn't uncommon in Parisian society, but actually seeing it, and being startled by it, made her feel priggish and unsophisticated.

The image of Guy bending down to kiss Victoire under her parasol came to her mind with agonizing clarity. Was this truly the type of woman he desired? Someone who was not only married, but was attending the party with another man?

A vise seemed to grip her throat. She was completely out of her depth, socializing with such people. The urge to flee and go back to her comfortable, uneventful life in Chartres overwhelmed her once more.

"Here are your drinks, *mesdames*," a servant said, carrying a silver tray with a glass of claret and a dram of a clear, greenish liqueur.

Claudine took both drinks and handed hers to Antonia. "Not a moment too soon. *Santé!*"

They clinked glasses, and Antonia took a sip of claret, looking out the window to watch the soothing evening light settle on the gardens. Suddenly, her neck prickled with awareness, as if someone was staring directly at her.

"You had better drink up, my dear," Claudine giggled. "Monsieur de Cazal has just arrived, and he seems quite eager to talk to you."

Chapter Three

ANTONIA NERVOUSLY TAPPED her fingertips against the rim of her glass. Why in God's name hadn't she taken up Claudine's offer of a stronger drink? Her nerves certainly could have used help to mellow them at the sight of Guy crossing the room in their direction.

When she'd first met him in the entrance hall, his disheveled attire had emphasized his rugged handsomeness, the strong lines of his jaw and his sinewy muscles. In formal evening wear, he was even more devastating: his clothes were subdued but impeccably tailored, and his royal blue jacket matched the color of his eyes in a way that made Antonia's chest bloom with jittery warmth. Obviously recovered from his shock at meeting her unexpectedly, he was now sporting a confident smile. Ten years had passed since she'd last seen him, and yet the roguish tilt of his full lips was stunningly familiar.

So was the uncomfortable thumping of her heart. She took another sip of claret and straightened her shoulders. *Be polite. Reply when spoken to. Nothing more.* No, she couldn't give him anything more.

"*Mesdames,*" he said smoothly when he'd reached their level. "I trust you're having a pleasant evening."

"Most assuredly, *monsieur,*" Claudine replied. "As you can see,

I am initiating Mademoiselle Saint Yves to the delights of *aperitivo*. And where is your pirate companion?"

Antonia raised her brows and Guy grinned. "Madame Rouget is referring to my friend, Nicolas Lefevre. If he were really a pirate, he would take less time dressing himself in the evening. As it is, he's certainly still in front of the mirror, choosing a waistcoat to match his breeches."

"Young men today are so very particular about the way they dress, aren't they? I must say, they were far less stylish when I was a girl. I should hire you and Monsieur Lefevre to give pointers to my sons!"

"You have sons then," Antonia said, eager to divert the conversation from Guy's outfits and, by extension, his good looks in general. "How many are you blessed with?"

"Four, and, believe me, they're most definitely not a blessing. The youngest is now fourteen and at school, but those lads burned through tutors and nannies quicker than flames through a haystack. Do you have any brothers?"

Jerome's face popped into her mind, wearing its habitual stern expression, and Antonia smiled wistfully. How she longed to see him again. He had every right to want to finish his apprenticeship, and he knew the family business was in good hands with Stanislas, but it simply wasn't the same without him there. She had more freedom, certainly, but the length of time it took for him to answer letters was a reminder of the distance that separated them.

Antonia had had enough distance to last a lifetime. No more. She was going to make the most of the here and now.

And that meant, in present circumstances, being closer to Guy than she could ever remember being. Was it her imagination, or was he leaning slightly toward her?

"Only one older brother," she replied, keeping a tight grip on her composure, "and he was always more serious and studious than my sister and I. But I have three young nephews now, and they are undoubtedly a handful."

"And you, *monsieur*?"

Guy's smile remained intact, but his gaze veiled ever so subtly. "I'm an only child. I have always been envious of Antonia's large family."

Her name rolling off his tongue sent a ripple down her spine. Not *Toinette*. Not *Mademoiselle Saint Yves*. Such a mark of intimacy between a man and a woman, even though they were acquainted since childhood, was bold indeed, yet Claudine didn't seem the least bit fazed.

Antonia gripped the stem of her glass, wavering between reproach and a sudden and irrepressible desire to hear him say it again. She took a sip of wine.

"That's right, Marie-Louise told me you both grew up in Chartres," Claudine said with a hint of curiosity in her tone. Was she aware of the full extent of their connection?

"We did," Guy replied. "I have known Antonia since we were children, and I can assure you her charms and grace have increased with every passing year."

Antonia nearly choked on her claret. What on earth was he doing, talking like that in front of her chaperone? For one dreadful moment, the thought occurred to her that he might be making fun of her, and it settled like a ball of lead in her stomach. But then his gaze swept over her, and her skin burned as if he'd touched her.

Claudine flicked her fan back and forth. "You are quite audacious, *monsieur*, but you have come to the right place for it."

They were interrupted by the arrival of a gentleman with curly blond hair. He was sporting a jaunty satin jacket and crimson breeches, and his angelic face was marred by a jagged scar crossing his brow.

"I see you're monopolizing the loveliest ladies in the room," he told Guy. "Nothing unusual there."

"Nicolas, allow me to introduce Mademoiselle Saint Yves," Guy said. "Antonia, this is my friend Nicolas Lefevre."

He bowed his head. His demeanor was both nonchalant and

inquisitive, and his green eyes glinted with mischief. "I've heard much about you, *mademoiselle*."

"I'm surprised, *monsieur*," Antonia replied. "I've only just returned from London a few months ago."

His lips curled into an enigmatic smile. "A great deal can happen in a short while."

Before she had time to ponder over his words, a servant came in the room to announce that dinner was served. François Aubertin gave a cheerful exclamation and Marie-Louise took his arm, and the guests started to pair off in a similar fashion to make their way to the dining room.

Nicolas turned to Claudine. "*Madame*, will you do me the honor?"

Claudine giggled and downed the remains of her glass in one gulp. "How could I possibly refuse a man whose breeches match the color of my dress?"

Antonia pressed her lips together. This inevitably meant that Guy would be escorting her.

"Shall we?" he said in a low voice, much too close to her ear.

She gave a stiff nod and set her glass down before placing her hand on his forearm. She intentionally kept her touch as light as possible, hoping it would ease her awareness of him, and barely grazed the soft material of his jacket with her fingertips.

"Madame Rouget is a character, is she not?" he asked pleasantly as they made the slow promenade to the attaining dining room.

"Indeed."

Instead of being vexed by her curt tone, Guy laughed softly, and the sound traveled all the way from her ear to the center of her body. "Have you always so detested small talk?"

"I don't detest it. I simply see no reason to elaborate when I agree with someone."

He raised an eyebrow teasingly. "Is that why you were always so quiet, because you agreed with everyone? I find that hard to believe."

His words stung more than they should have. It figured her shyness would be her defining feature—nay, her *only* feature in his eyes.

"I had more than my share of small talk when I was a paid companion in London," she retorted. "Hours and hours on end chatting about nothing. It was enough to last a lifetime."

That washed the mirth from his face and gave him pause. "You were a paid companion?"

"I was lucky to get the position. Honorine took care of the household and the children—when we arrived in London, she was pregnant with Marie, and Jeanne was only a year old. The rest of us had to earn money. Jerome and Stanislas worked as masons, and as for me… It was either that or become a maid."

And she had been grateful for it. She had been spared working her hands raw and bruising her knees scrubbing floors. Not to mention that employers were said to have a particular taste for French maids, who were reputed to be less inhibited than their British counterparts. But oh, those afternoons spent sitting in bleak, dimly lit rooms, trying to stave off the chill with a threadbare blanket, listening to the monotonous drone of a widow whose main occupation was to criticize the help…

For a moment, Guy looked like he wanted to ask her more questions, but his expression slid back into polished suavity. "In that case, I'll endeavor to be as silent as possible when I'm in your company."

A tinge of guilt she couldn't brush away crept on the edge of her mind. True, she didn't want to fall at his feet in childish adoration, but how could she truly gauge his character if she didn't even give him a chance to talk to her?

"Please don't," she said with a sigh. "I simply wish we could discuss things in earnest. After all, we are not strangers."

"No, we are not," Guy said in a curious tone that Antonia couldn't quite interpret. "Well, if we are seated together, you'll be free to interrogate me at your leisure."

They finally entered the immense dining room, and Antonia

was momentarily stunned by its opulence. It was long enough to fit a table that would seat the fifty or so guests, and in spite of Marie-Louise's claims that the ambiance of the house party was informal, chandeliers, crystal glasses and polished silverware gleamed in perfectly ordered rows on the white linen tablecloth.

Marie-Louise approached them to direct them to their seat. "Claudine has requested you sit next to her, my dear," she said, addressing Antonia. "And you, *monsieur*, at the head of the table with us. Victoire told me you were wondering who sired the steed you rode today, and my husband has been dying to talk someone's ear off about horse breeding."

"I would be honored," Guy replied, then turned to Antonia. "I suppose the interrogation will have to wait."

Antonia couldn't quite tell if he was relieved or disappointed. But when her hand slipped from his arm, the sensation of loss was unmistakable.

DAMN VICTOIRE AND her schemes.

Guy swirled the dregs of Montrachet at the bottom of his glass as François blathered on about the Godolphin Arabian— nothing he didn't know already. He glanced up and caught his angelic beauty looking at him with a devilish smile from the other side of the table. The minx, she must be thoroughly enjoying the sight of him stuck next to François when Antonia sat several place-settings away.

You didn't think it would be that easy, did you? she seemed to be taunting him.

Pity for her, it only made him more determined. He'd finally managed to have some semblance of discussion with Antonia and he wasn't going to stop there.

After what seemed like hours, platters of candied fruit were served to conclude the meal and they finally rose from the table.

Guy watched Claudine link her arm with Antonia's, no doubt bringing her to the card room. He held back, however, and joined other guests in the billiards room, where it was customary for the gentlemen to play, smoke and honor François's ample reserves of cognac.

As he sipped his cognac, comfortably sprawled on an armchair of plush green velvet that matched the dark autumnal tones of the room, Guy let his thoughts stray back to Antonia. So far flirting with her was both easier and harder than he'd expected. Harder, because her adolescent shyness had transformed over the years into a shell of reserve that took much more than a charming smile and a few courteous words to crack. Easier, because any red-blooded man would enjoy winning the favor of such a desirable young woman. The silky curls, the slim neck circled with gleaming pearls, and those soft, luscious curves that he couldn't help but want to touch, grab, sink into... The image of shy little Toinette was rapidly and definitively fading from his mind, giving way to the very palpable appeal Antonia held in the present. An appeal she was seemingly unaware of, which made the temptation all the more maddening.

No, he wouldn't have to force himself one bit when it would come to luring her into his arms and taking her to bed.

"Elaborating your battle plan for the evening?"

Nicolas dropped down in the chair next to his with a sigh of content. Guy stretched out his glass to clink it with his, and both of them took a sip.

"No battle plan," Guy said. "Talking is good enough for the time being."

"I suppose a girl like that requires one to walk on eggshells."

"A girl like what?"

"Sweet. Candid." Nicolas wrinkled his nose. "*Virginal.*"

True, Antonia was almost certainly a virgin, yet Guy couldn't match Nicolas's words with her character. Something about her—the way she held herself, perhaps, or the grave depths of her eyes, especially when she was lost in her own thoughts—told him she wasn't the type of naive lamb Nicolas scorned.

"I've told you this before, Lefevre, virginity isn't a personality trait. There's no reason Antonia should be less passionate than any other woman. She might simply be better at hiding it."

"Unlike Victoire, who flaunts her appetites as if they were the bloody Tricolore on a barricade."

Guy couldn't argue with that; the first time he'd seen Victoire, in one of the racier salons of the capital, she'd been posing as Marianne in a satirical *tableau vivant*, baring one breast to the laudatory crowd. Had De Brienne been present that night? He couldn't recall. Imagining himself in the same position, a besotted lover looking on without a word as his mistress exposed her bosom to a throng of drunken party guests, made the taste of his cognac sour. Good Lord, was he really that much of a prude?

"There is something to be said about the thrill of surprise," he said, as much for Nicolas as for himself. "Like unwrapping a gift. Even if you end up disappointed, there's always that riveting moment when you're eager to see what's inside."

"I usually know what I'm going to see when I lift a woman's skirts," Nicolas smirked. "Nothing worth the considerable trouble of seducing an innocent."

Guy finished his glass and stood up. "An indolent through and through. Well, if you'll excuse me, I'm going to put my evening to good use."

Nicolas slumped further in the chair and crossed his long legs in front of him. "Happy hunting, my friend."

Guy left the billiards room and strolled toward the cards room, where many of the guests had assembled to play. Claudine was sitting at a small table next to Marie-Louise, nodding her head as she started to doze off. The bay windows opened on the terrace, letting a soft breeze waft inside as moths started to flutter around the lamps.

Antonia was standing on the terrace, her hands on the stone balustrade, staring out into the night. The simple elegance of the vision before him struck him in a strange way, as if his heart couldn't quite settle in its place from one beat to the next. He stepped outside and approached her slowly. When she heard him, she turned around, her lips slightly parted.

"Here you are," he said. "May I join you?"

"You were looking for me?"

He titled his head. "You sound surprised. Is it really so strange, after you told me you wished we could talk?"

She wrapped her stole a bit tighter around her shoulders, the golden glow coming from inside illuminating one half of her lovely face. "Better now than at the dinner table. I'm glad we have a little privacy."

A little, but not nearly enough for what he'd like to do. Touch the errant curl at her temple. Slide his hand down the curve of her neck. Step closer, much closer, than where he was now.

Pace yourself. Go easy. Antonia had just now started to relax around him. No need to make her skittish again.

"There are certain things… which are difficult to say in public," she continued. "I wanted to send you a letter, actually, but I did not know where to reach you."

Was she referring to their betrothal? The thumping in his chest grew more acute. "I'm listening."

Antonia lowered her gaze. "I was very sorry to hear about your parents. We all were. What a terrible trial it must have been for you."

He watched her intently, his throat constricting. How had she found out? *Lazare Fournier.* Yes, of course. Fournier had been his father's most trusted employee at the bank, and he was currently trying to get it running again. He had closely followed Guy's attempts to retrieve the assets and properties which had been confiscated by the Revolutionary Tribunal and they had exchanged several letters, one of which mentioned the return of the Saint Yves family to Chartres. Fournier must have told them that Monsieur and Madame de Cazal were dead.

Just as well that Guy had stopped replying to his missives,

despite the urgency of Fournier's pleas. Chartres was far away, but the past was still too close for him to want to delve into it.

"Yes, well," he said curtly. "No more a trial than it was for you when your parents passed."

"It's not the same. Jerome was there to take care of me. Honorine and Stanislas as well. Besides, looking back, I take comfort in the fact that they weren't forced into exile with the rest of us."

Antonia's parents had succumbed to a febrile illness a few days apart, just as the Reign of Terror was tightening like a noose around them. At the time, hearing the news, he'd been filled with sorrow and gratitude that his own family had been spared. The fever that had swept through Chartres that winter had claimed its share of victims.

Now he saw it as a mercy. At least they had died in their beds.

"How did it happen?" Antonia asked gently.

"Does it really matter how?" he snapped.

She startled and he gripped the balustrade to regain his bearings. The hurt, the pain, the darkness, it was bubbling up in his chest again, squeezing his lungs. He forced himself to take a deep breath and glanced inside. The players' exclamations and the cheerful shuffling of cards comforted him. It was fine. *He* was fine.

"We were in Geneva, staying with relatives," he explained in a milder tone. "I could bore you with the details, but there is nothing much to be said about the dull life we led there. I came back alone. That's it."

"And you went to Paris?"

Her large gray eyes filled with melancholy. Had she waited for him to come back, only to be disappointed when he didn't? Something within him stirred at the thought of Antonia staring out her window at the road in front of the Saint Yves house. To have someone longing for him, a home to return to…

He shook the image away. "I've had to appeal to the administration of the Consulate to get some of our holdings back. It's a lengthy process."

A process that had come to fruition some months ago, but it was simpler to let her believe this was the reason he had not yet returned. Any other reason he could give her, she would not understand. How could she? She had not the faintest idea of the temptations a city like Paris presented. Nor how easy it was to numb the pain with a constant stream of pleasures.

Antonia smiled, but it didn't chase the sorrow in her gaze. "It looks like you made a life for yourself there. That's another thing I wanted to talk to you about. Seeing as our parents are now deceased, there's no reason why we shouldn't decide, as adults..."

She inhaled sharply and retreated again into that cold, formal constraint. Without moving, she seemed to have withdrawn beyond reach, and he had the sudden impulse to grab her wrist, pull her back, shake her out of it.

"The betrothal they arranged between us has no legal bearing, and no reason to be maintained," she concluded. "Especially if you have... an *understanding* with someone else."

Guy frowned. "An understanding? Whatever gave you that idea?"

Antonia didn't answer but shifted uncomfortably. Could it be that she had seen him promenading with Victoire that afternoon? Or worse, witnessed from afar the moment where Victoire had shielded them with her parasol, offering her lips to him? His fists clenched. Damn his foolishness. From now on he would stay far, far away from that particular temptation.

"I assure you, there is nothing of the sort," he said evenly. "But let us put aside our parents' accord for the time being. Can we not simply get reacquainted, you and I?"

"As friends, you mean. Nothing more."

Her choice of words piqued him. To be so bluntly disregarded as a viable prospect made his blood boil with the urge to prove her wrong.

"Friends," he agreed with an affable smile.

For now.

Chapter Four

THE GOLDEN GRASS hummed with insects as the morning sun blazed ever more ruthlessly over the fields. Antonia loosened her embroidered fichu; the few early risers had set off for a walk in the neighboring countryside, but it was already uncomfortably hot. The brim of her straw hat—the same with which she helped out in the vegetable garden back in Chartres—provided the only shade. When one's hands were always busy, a parasol was a useless luxury. She could certainly use one now, however. If she stayed out in the sun much longer, her arms would freckle.

"Are you all right, Mademoiselle Saint Yves?"

Guy had stopped further down the path and turned to call to her. With no apparent effort, he had led the group, but kept himself from walking at too brisk a pace for the others. Riding, fencing, climbing: clear memories of his apparently effortless talent for athletics surfaced in her mind. He had always teemed with an endless supply of restless energy.

"Perfectly well, thank you," she called in response.

He stood his ground. Why was he waiting for her? Her silly heart clamored an even sillier answer, but she muffled it mercilessly. Guy was just being polite and would have done the same for any other woman of his acquaintance. He was courteously respecting her request that they resume a perfectly proper friendship, which was what she wished.

Liar.

Antonia tucked her fichu back in place. Guy watched her descend the path without betraying any sign of being in a hurry, but she accelerated nonetheless. If they strayed too far from the rest of the group, people would take notice.

"Oof!"

The sole of her shoe slid on a smooth stone and she tripped forward, arms outstretched. Guy leaped to catch her, his hands firmly grasping her forearms. She struggled to steady herself, mortification burning over her face with more force than the scorching sun. What if he thought she had done it on purpose?

His hands lingered for a moment on the sensitive skin of her wrists before letting go, and her mortification turned to agitation. These little incidents had been happening with increasing frequency over the past three days. A gaze held a second too long. A word murmured a bit too close to her ear. A brush of his fingers against the small of her back, so light she wondered if she had imagined it. But Guy was so unfailingly cordial the rest of the time that she refused to let herself believe he was trying to charm her.

She crossed her arms over her chest. "Forgive me. That was clumsy of me."

Guy reached over to straighten her hat. "You ought to be more careful, Antonia."

And then there were the moments when he still called her by her name, moments when no one else could hear him and there was no need for propriety, and oh, how she longed for his deep, masculine voice saying the word, and how she hated herself for it.

"Right. Shall we catch up with the others?" she asked with forced enthusiasm.

She started again without waiting for his answer and he followed, his hands behind his back. "You've got endurance. Do you walk often back home?"

"Whenever I can, which isn't often," she replied with a rueful smile. "It's hard work helping Honorine around the house and with the children. But I do enjoy it, and I missed it dearly when we were in London. Walking in the city is a necessity, not a recreation."

"Don't they have parks and the like in London?"

"They do, though I wasn't often at my leisure to visit them. I went to Hyde Park a few times, but it's not the same."

She stopped to look at the landscape of low hills and woods that rolled smoothly toward Verneuil, and breathed the scent of wildflowers and hay ready for threshing. No, the city would never compare to the countryside.

"What about you?" she asked as they continued. "You're so fond of riding, I imagine it's difficult to do as much as you'd like in Paris."

"I'll admit, there aren't many places besides the Champs Élysées where a horse can stretch its legs. I've taken up *savate* to keep my form."

"*Savate*? What's that?"

"I suggest you ask Nicolas," he replied with a hint of mischief. "He's the one who introduced me to it. But I'm warning you, it involves quite a lot of punching and kicking. A respectable lady such as yourself might not approve."

His rumbling tone and the warmth that curled in her stomach was making her feel anything but respectable. Thankfully, they had caught up with the rest of the guests and immediately, Guy joined in their discussion about Aubertin's plans to modernize their estate.

"It's a new century," Guy said when one of the men asked him for his opinion on the new threshing machine being developed in Britain. "We would be fools to let the habits of the previous one hold us back, even if that means taking some risks."

Antonia found herself admiring how eloquently he expressed himself, his obvious ease at being the center of attention, the flame that grew in his deep blue eyes when he spoke with conviction. With a start, she realized he reminded her of his father, Joseph de Cazal, when he argued and debated with her own father at the dinner table. No doubt Guy would make an exceptional leader if he managed to get the bank on its feet again.

Steeling her heart from crossing the fine line between admiration and adoration, she forced her gaze away from him and increased her pace to pass the main group and forge ahead. By the time she had reached the chateau, she was breathless, but better it be from walking too fast than from hearing Guy discuss the latest innovations in efficient plowing.

"There you are, my dear," Claudine called from the terrace. "I saw you arriving from the window! Come inside to cool off, it's boiling out here!"

Antonia smiled and gave her a little wave. Though no closer to acting as a chaperone than when they'd first met, Claudine was steadfast in her companionship and generously helped Antonia navigate the unfamiliar waters of the fashionable set. She was also highly entertaining.

As soon as Antonia reached the terrace, Claudine slipped an arm into hers and they went inside. The cool inside air washed over Antonia and she took off her hat with a sigh of relief.

"I've been positively dying of boredom since I came down half an hour ago and noticed you were gone," Claudine said as they made their way to the sitting room. "Marie-Louise is still sleeping, but that's no surprise, she's never up before noon if she can help it…"

Claudine chattered on, and Antonia let herself be lulled into the comfort of the brightly lit room decorated in shades of pink and yellow that reminded her of freshly baked macarons. The women assembled there to enjoy refreshments and catch up on their needlework, as well as the latest gossip. As Antonia didn't know any of the people they mentioned, she was free to simply sit in silence and let her thoughts drift as she worked on a ribbon of embroidered flowers for Jeanne.

"So, was Monsieur de Cazal with you this morning?" Claudine murmured, her hoop cast aside on the divan, as usual.

"He was," Antonia replied. Was that a snag in her voice? She cleared her throat needlessly. "There were seven of us in total."

A sly little smile played on Claudine's mouth and she glanced toward the two other ladies present, who were engrossed in a conversation about how much their respective modistes charged for an evening dress. "I'm not surprised he was among the early risers," she continued, "though I've heard he keeps quite a different schedule in the city."

"Is that so?" Antonia hated to fish for information in this manner, but Claudine was apparently ready to offer it up on a silver platter.

"If Marie-Louise is to be believed, Guy and his charming friend Nicolas are quite the night owls. They don't have the clout or the money to be invited to the salons of Juliette Récamier or Madame de Condorcet."

Indeed. These salons were the gathering place of France's intellectual elite, and so famous even Antonia had heard of them.

Claudine lowered her tone. "However, they're doing very well for themselves in more... shall we say, *lively* venues."

"Lively? In what sense?"

"My dear, I would be loathe to shock you with too detailed descriptions of what goes on in certain salons. And after all, it is only hearsay. But apparently, these two gentlemen have had quite an impressive number of conquests between them. Some even claim there are a few ladies who have had the pleasure to sample both."

Antonia pricked her forefinger with her needle and gave a little yelp. "*Both?*"

Surely Claudine couldn't mean at the same time. That sort of thing would be simply too appalling to contemplate. But even so, there was no mistaking what kind of life Guy was leading in Paris.

"Are you saying that Guy is a... a..."

"A *débauché?*" Claudine completed. "Oh no, my dear, rest assured he isn't. I've met more than a few in my days, believe me, and you can always tell a true *débauché* by the look in his eyes. Cold, cynical, malicious. It's a state of mind rather than a state of affairs."

Antonia furiously concentrated on the intricate flower she was stitching. No, Guy's eyes weren't cold. Quite the opposite, actually, especially when they landed on her. She squirmed discreetly in her seat, trying to alleviate some of the pressure that settled low in her belly.

"However, it's only natural that a vigorous young man such as himself should seek sport to channel his ardor. He's a charmer, certainly, but I cannot imagine such a man has to force his attentions on anyone."

Overtaken with a flush of heat, Antonia set her work down to pour herself a glass of water from the silver carafe sitting on a side table. Claudine's words were bringing wicked, forbidden images to her mind which she was powerless to stave off. When she was a girl, pining after him, her fantasies had never strayed beyond a moonlit kiss and a declaration of love, exciting her into a flurry of emotions that made her feel like the heroine of one of her beloved sentimental novels.

Now older and wiser, she had thought herself pragmatic enough to know the difference between a novel and reality. Having heard Honorine and other ladies describe the pleasures of the marital bed, or any bed for that matter, she also knew where such kisses led to, though beyond the begetting of children, the completion of the act itself remained elusive.

Why was it, then, that she couldn't help picturing Guy pulling her away from the path they'd tread that morning to the privacy of a thicket, wrapping his arms around her waist, pressing his mouth to hers, caressing her where the flush was most pressing with his strong, sure hands?

"Are you well, my dear?" Claudine asked after Antonia had emptied the glass in long, slow gulps. "I hope the sun didn't get to you. With your lovely complexion you must take care."

At that moment, a trio of ladies entered the room and the

conversation veered toward more acceptable topics. Antonia returned to her embroidery, relieved but disquieted. The need she felt couldn't be quenched with water, nor silenced with reasonable words; it lay simmering in the back of her mind, momentarily tamed, but ready to flare up again if she let it.

⇶⫷

"WHICH STUFFY ROMAN scholar wrote that Amazons cut off one breast to shoot arrows?"

Guy glanced back at Nicolas, who was reclining lazily on his chair, a pencil and paper in hand. An archery range had been set up on the flat expanse of lawn in front of the chateau's southern facade. One of the young ladies had just taken her turn, stretching her arm back to tauten the bowstring and giving them an unfettered view of her generous bosom.

"I was never much interested in the classics, I'm afraid," Guy replied.

"Well, whoever the fool was, he was mistaken. See, it's perfectly possible to shoot with both."

She let go of the bowstring, and the arrow landed with a thump on the left side of the target a few meters away. The guests clapped politely, and Nicolas jotted a number down.

Victoire rose from the wicker divan she was sharing with De Brienne and strode forward. "I believe I'm next."

She removed her hat, handing it to a nearby footman, and took the bow. In her form-fitting white dress, her golden curls gleaming in the vibrant sunlight of the late afternoon, she looked like Diana herself descended from the heavens to the mortal realm. Her movements were graceful and firm, her position flawless. *Thwack.* The arrow shot straight into the bullseye.

This time, the applause was more than polite. Victoire smiled sweetly, but there was a blaze of arrogance in her gaze that Guy had seen many times before, the one that came with the unanimous acceptance that she was the best. They had impro-vised a tournament of sorts, keeping a tally of points as each archer took a turn and wagering on the outcome, and so far she was ahead.

"Splendid, *madame*," Nicolas said. "Had you been born a few centuries earlier, you would've made the barbarian hordes tremble."

"I rather think so, yes," she replied lightly. "Is it not your turn, Monsieur de Cazal?"

Guy nodded and stood. Given the heat and the need for am-ple movement, the gentlemen had taken off their jackets and cravats, remaining in shirt and waistcoat. He stretched his long arms leisurely, itching for a chance to best Victoire's score.

"Was it not a splendid idea for the afternoon's entertain-ment?" she teased, handing him the bow. "Such a shame your little friend isn't joining in."

She glanced over his shoulder, and he followed her gaze to where Antonia was sitting with Claudine, Marie-Louise and other matrons, safely tucked away under the shade of a dais a little further away. If there was anything that Antonia was sure not to take part in, it was a sport where one had to display individual skill in front of a crowd.

He turned back to Victoire. "You know, I can't decide what pleased you more when you suggested an archery tournament: the idea of everyone admiring your silhouette when you shoot, or the certainty that you would halt me in my efforts to obtain Antonia's good graces for a few hours."

He positioned himself, firmly placing his fingers on the bow and pulling the string back in one swift, unhesitating movement before releasing. *Thunk.* Another bullseye, right next to Victoire's arrow.

"I am not at fault here," she said with mock innocence. "If the foolish girl wanted to break free from that flock of hens, nothing would prevent her from doing so."

Something in her tone poked at him, made him want to

prove her wrong and see that pretty, provocative smile of hers turn into a grimace. He handed the bow back to her and stalked away toward the dais.

"Well met, old fellow," Nicolas said as Guy passed next to him. "You never miss your mark when you've got your eye on the prize."

Bolstered by his friend's sly encouragement, Guy relaxed his expression into one of charming nonchalance as he approached the group of ladies who were watching the archers amid a flutter of fans.

"Mademoiselle Saint Yves," he addressed her. In spite of the straw hat safely tied on her head whenever she went outside, the sun had managed to leave a rosy glow on her cheeks during their walk that morning. By God, she was as lovely and tempting as a golden Reinette apple. "Would you care to take a turn?"

"It's kind of you to offer," Antonia replied, fidgeting with the thin peach muslin of her dress, "but I wouldn't want to intrude on your tournament. Besides, I've never tried archery before."

He had guessed as much. That wasn't going to stop him, on the contrary.

"Then this is the perfect opportunity, is it not?"

"Perhaps another time, when you're not playing to win…"

He lifted his shoulders. "I'll tell Nicolas not to tally your points. It's all very informal."

"I've placed my bet on you, *monsieur*," Marie-Louise said cheerfully. "You're quite the marksman, aren't you? Though I do believe you're a few points shy of Victoire."

"Sadly, you are correct, but convincing Mademoiselle Saint Yves to have a turn would be a victory in itself."

Antonia gnawed at her bottom lip, still unsure. "I… I would not even know how to hold the bow…"

"I'll show you," he said offhandedly, though his heart gave a little jolt. "It's not complicated, you'll see."

"Oh, do try, my dear," Claudine pitched in, squeezing her hand. "We'll all be cheering for you, and I the loudest."

Antonia's eyes met his, and for a moment, he was mesmerized by the depths of longing he found there, as if she was yearning to break free from whatever was holding her back, and not just when it came to a silly archery tournament. But it vanished as soon as she rose to her feet. Claudine clapped happily and a smile fought its way to Antonia's mouth.

Guy offered her his arm and walked her to where De Brienne had just finished shooting.

"Madame Le Plessis is still ahead," Nicolas announced, glancing down at his paper, "with Monsieur de Cazal a close second, Monsieur de Brienne third, and the rest of you valiantly trailing behind."

"Hold the tally for a moment, will you?" Guy asked. "Mademoiselle Saint Yves wants a go."

"Certainly."

Guy glanced at Victoire, who was waiting for De Brienne on the divan. She watched them with practiced indifference that betrayed her displeasure. She probably hadn't counted on him being so insistent with Antonia, nor on Antonia relinquishing her comfortable spot in the shade to risk embarrassment. And thus she had unwittingly presented him with the perfect opportunity to further his cause.

"Take off your hat," he told Antonia. "Just for a moment, so it doesn't get in the way. The sun has lost its glare at this hour."

She nodded and tugged nervously at the faded ribbons. "Will you hold it for me?"

He took the hat but immediately handed it over to a footman. "I'd rather keep my hands free, in case I need to assist you."

The glow on her cheeks intensified. "Oh. I see."

"Here," he said, taking the bow from the small wooden table where it lay, and that served as the placement mark. "Start by gripping it in your left hand and hold the arrow in your right…"

Meticulously, without touching her, he instructed her on the correct way to lift the bow and position the arrow. Centimeter by centimeter, he drew closer, until the scent of honeysuckle drifted to him, a subtle and feminine perfume he had learned to recognize as uniquely hers in the past days.

"Lift your elbow just a bit…"

He lightly tapped the underside of her arm to correct her and felt the slightest of shivers.

"Right." His tone was raspy, roughened by the sensations that were starting to build up within him. "Spread your legs and, ah…"

"Like this?"

"Yes." He swallowed against the hammering pulse in his chest. "Plant your feet firmly on the ground to keep your balance and draw the string back."

Antonia complied, though her arm shook from the effort and she struggled to steady the butt of the arrow. Guy placed his hands over hers to help, and for one glorious moment, he enveloped her in his embrace, the feel of her body saturating his senses. She gave a halting breath and from where he stood, he could see the top of her breasts straining against her bodice under the delicate fichu. Mercy, this was the sweetest torture, but if he didn't control himself, he would step away with a rather visible problem.

"When should I let go?" she asked in a murmur.

His cheek nearly brushed against the silk of her hair. "Now, Antonia."

Together, they released the string and the arrow went zooming forward, planting itself at the very edge of the target.

Guy pulled back as a patter of applause rose from the crowd. "Wonderful. Well done."

Antonia turned to him, her breathing still a bit uneven but beaming with pleasure. "Yes, that was… rather invigorating."

Any more so and he would have laid her down on the lawn in front of everyone to kiss her senseless. "I'm glad you think so."

"Bravo, *mademoiselle*," Nicolas called out. "Hitting the target on your first try, that shows remarkable aptitude for a novice. Wouldn't you say so, Guy?"

Guy raised an eyebrow at his friend's loaded tone, but Nicolas simply grinned.

"Whose turn is it now?" Victoire demanded impatiently.

Antonia scrambled to set the bow back on the table, but Guy pointedly refused to look at Victoire. For some reason, he no longer cared about vexing her. He simply wanted to make Antonia's enjoyment last as long as possible.

"*Seigneur!*"

There was a high-pitched cry, followed immediately by the clatter of two chairs falling to the ground. They looked to the dais and Antonia's smile vanished. Claudine had slumped from her seat to the lawn.

"She's fainted!" Marie-Louise exclaimed. "Please, someone come help!"

Chapter Five

"WHAT HAPPENED?"

"Splash some water on her face!"

"It's her stays. She's laced them too tightly."

The guests gathered around Claudine's limp form, and Antonia watched helplessly as François knelt on the grass beside her, gently tapping her cheek.

"Is she still breathing?" Marie-Louise sniffled. "Oh, this is all my fault! I should have had the claret chilled before serving it, the heat wouldn't have gotten to her then."

"Calm yourself, my love," François said. "Her breathing is even and her pulse is strong. Probably just a brief malaise."

Antonia bit her lip, clutching her hands together. Suddenly, a warm, comforting presence materialized behind her. She didn't need to look around to know it was—Guy, catching up with her after she'd run in all haste across the lawn, and a sliver of longing cut through her worry.

"Let's see if this helps…"

François took a small silver flask from his waistcoat pocket, unscrewed the lid and held it under Claudine's nose. She stirred faintly, then blinked. A hum passed through the crowd and Marie-Louise sniffled even louder.

"François has always claimed cognac can cure any ailment,"

Guy murmured next to Antonia's ear. He was unbearably close, his chest almost touching her back, and she was starting to feel quite light-headed herself. "I suppose this proves him right."

"Oh, but she's still quite pale." She drew her attention back to her friend, who was being helped into a sitting position.

François took the glass that Marie-Louise handed to him, which was filled with clear liquid Antonia hoped to God was water and not genever. "Here, drink this."

Claudine took a few sips and appeared to be gathering her spirits, but her arms remained limp at her sides.

"We must get her inside so she can rest." Antonia stepped forward and sank to her knees next to her. "Claudine, are you well enough to stand?"

"I shall try," she replied in a thin voice.

Antonia clasped her hands and helped her to her feet, but Claudine wavered. François steadied her and put her arm around her neck to support her weight.

"I will accompany her back to the chateau," he said.

"But, my love, your knee!" Marie-Louise exclaimed. "You know what the physician told you after your fall. No strenuous exercise for three months if you want to ride again."

Antonia thought Claudine might object to being referred to as *strenuous exercise*, but in truth, François's face was already turning crimson from the effort.

"I'll do it," Guy offered, and took his place with significantly more ease. "Come, Antonia."

"What about the tournament?" Victoire's displeased voice rang out sharply. "Are we to simply wait and twiddle our thumbs until you return?"

"Continue without me," Guy replied shortly. "I forfeit."

And with that, he started toward the chateau, letting Claudine set the pace as she set one foot in front of the other.

"Well, Madame Le Plessis, it's you against De Brienne now, fancy that," Antonia heard Nicolas say as she gathered Claudine's fan and hat before following them.

By the time they arrived at the chateau, Claudine was walking with more assurance, though still very slowly. Antonia asked the *majordome* to send for her maid, and they carefully ascended the stairs before turning in the darkened corridor of the east wing.

"You must accept my most heartfelt thanks and apologies, *monsieur*," Claudine said in a trembling voice. "I just don't know what came over me! One minute I was watching Antonia's impressive performance, and the next…"

Antonia blushed at the mention of her turn with the bow, the ghost of Guy's hands over hers still lingering on her skin, but Guy simply smiled. "Next time, I would suggest you drink one glass of water between each glass of claret or cider if you mean to parch your thirst. It will keep you properly sustained."

"Are you saying I wilted like a flower? How poetic."

They had arrived in front of her room and Guy delicately let her go.

"I'll stay with her," Antonia told him. "You may go back outside if you wish."

He frowned and gave no reply. Disconcerted, Antonia led Claudine inside her room and closed the door behind them.

When her maid undressed her and untied her stays, leaving her in her chemise, Claudine gave a great sigh of relief.

"Would you like me to read to you?" Antonia asked as her friend lay down on her bed.

Claudine patted her hand. "How very sweet you are. But I am so drowsy now, I feel like I could sleep for a hundred years, and even the kiss of a handsome prince wouldn't wake me."

"Very well. I shall return in the evening to see if you are feeling better."

"Mmmmhyes," she mumbled, already half asleep.

Antonia closed the curtains to plunge the room in a soothing shade, then quietly left, marveling at how quickly her friend had sunk into slumber.

Guy was waiting for her in the corridor, and a little ripple of delight coursed through her. "How is she?"

"Sleeping like a babe," she replied with a smile. "I have no doubt she'll be replenished in a few hours, when it's time for *aperitivo*."

He grinned and they started slowly back toward the staircase. Antonia shivered, struck with how very alone they were at that moment. Alone and unchaperoned, with the only light filtering from the spaces in the shutters which the servants had closed to ward off the sun's glare. The dimness enveloped them like a blanket and whispered temptingly in her ear that whatever happened here would remain a secret.

"She's taken quite a liking to you."

Why did the low timbre of his voice make her want to bolt down the corridor and halt at the same time? His proximity, the refreshing dimness surrounding them, all of it was making her lose her senses, and she must regain them before she said or did something catastrophically stupid. Yet she couldn't bring her feet to pick up the pace. She wanted him near. She wanted the corridor to go on forever.

"Claudine is a merry, generous spirit," she replied. "I don't think there's anyone she doesn't like."

"No, it's just that..." he insisted. "Some may look down on her for being so spontaneous in her reactions, even brush her off as ridiculous, but not so with you. She recognizes your worth. Your lack of pretension." He took her hand in his and stopped to face her. "Your kind heart."

Antonia looked down at his fingers gripping hers, her heart suddenly pounding so hard it knocked the breath out of her lungs. He released her, but she remained frozen in place.

She inhaled sharply to find her voice again. "You're the one who showed kindness in forfeiting the tournament."

"Think nothing of it. It was just a silly game."

"Not so silly. When we—when I shot the arrow and it hit its mark, I immediately understood its appeal. I didn't expect it to be so riveting."

"Neither did I."

His tone ran deeper now, lush as velvet. She dared meet his eye, and her knees nearly buckled. Guy was looking at her as if she was a glass of cold water he meant to drink to the very last drop.

"Well, I'm sure the tournament isn't over yet," she blurted out, because he couldn't, simply *couldn't* be looking at her that way, not in this dark empty corridor with the feel of his arms around her still burning in her mind. "If you hurry, you can catch up."

"I'd rather stay here."

She rambled on, desperately trying to fill the space between them to dissipate the crackling tension. "Understandably, staying outside for too long can be wearisome in this heat, it's so much cooler indoors."

He stepped forward and reached out to touch one of the many curls that had escaped from her chignon, idly bringing it back behind her ear. "If I wanted to cool down, I would make a better job of it out in the blazing sun."

She opened her mouth to reply, but she was out of words. His gaze was penetrating, enticing, flowing from her eyes to land on her mouth, her breasts. He stroked another curl, but this time his hand lingered to cup her face, and his thumb lightly traced over her lower lip. Her eyes fluttered shut.

His lips touched hers, feather-light. She froze. Guy was kissing her. *Guy.* How was she to respond? She'd never been kissed before. Surely he would sense her inexperience and draw back. Her limbs trembled as she stood petrified, too nervous to move.

Guy pressed a small kiss on the corner of her mouth, then the other. "Don't fret," he murmured. "I shall do nothing that displeases you."

"It's not that, but I… I have never…"

He mouth curled into a smile. "No matter. I can teach you this as well. You need only follow my lead."

His lips melded with hers again and Antonia closed her eyes, giving herself over to the sensation. She placed her hands on his toned chest and met the movement of his mouth with her own, hesitantly at first, then more ardently. A moan resounded in the back of his throat and he opened his mouth slightly to touch his tongue with hers. Oh, that was… strange, but right. So incredibly right that her head whirled. Obeying her body's natural impulse, she did the same, melting into the flick of his tongue.

He smelled of the outdoors, of fresh grass and sunbaked linen, and the scent and taste and feel of him made her want to break free of all doubts and restrictions. Parting her mouth to his tongue's heated caress was like the thrill of the arrow being released, all potential until it drove deep into the target, like running wild and unfettered on a summer's day.

She gripped the lapels of his shirt to steady herself, and his hands moved to encircle her waist, pulling her against the imposing hardness in his breeches. A jolt of shock seized her, but quickly mellowed into a pulsing warmth.

One kiss rolled seamlessly into another, relentlessly increasing the delicious pressure between her thighs, driving her to arch against the firm length that might assuage it. Guy groaned again and his mouth strayed downward to her neck. When he nipped the delicate skin, she couldn't help a whimper of pleasure.

"Antonia," he rasped. "Sweet, lovely Antonia…"

The words cut through her, all the way to a memory laying in the back of her mind, drawing new blood from a closed wound. Her eyes flew open and she pushed Guy back.

He stepped back, chest heaving, his gaze a blue storm of arousal and confusion.

"I—I can't," she stammered. "I'm sorry. I…"

Desire roared in her pulse still, an angry animal being forced back into a cage. She turned away from him and fled back to the staircase and the dazzling sunshine. Before she could push them away, vivid images flashed before her.

A moonlit garden. Rose bushes. A gazebo. A young girl in a white dress with a pink sash who fancied herself the heroine of a sentimental novel, staring up at the starlit sky.

And then, whispers coming from the gazebo. She should have stifled her curiosity, gone back inside. She shouldn't have tiptoed nearer and crouched down to hear what was being said.

Oh Guy, how wicked you are! Should you be doing this, the very night of your betrothal?

This so-called betrothal is preposterous. Me, marry Toinette? Have you seen her? She's a child. Half the time she's tripping over her words, and the other half, she's got her nose buried in a book.

Perhaps better to hide those unsightly spots.

A dainty giggle and a deep chuckle that rang, to her ears, like a funeral bell. *I'm telling you, it's an absurd fancy, no doubt concocted by our mothers. When I do marry, it certainly won't be with the likes of her.*

Then a different sound altogether, muffled and wet and forbidden. They were kissing, while her heart lay broken at her feet.

Sweet, lovely Aurélie…

Antonia clutched the polished banister. She had arrived at the bottom of the stairs. Words whispered to another, so long ago, had been repeated to her not a minute past. But if she pursued this madness and let her heart be broken again, this time there would be no mending it.

⇛⇚

Guy stood in the empty corridor, dumbstruck, struggling to control his winded breath and frenzied lust. What the devil had just happened?

He stumbled back toward the wall and bent forward, clutching his knees. It would take a few moments for his hardened cock to catch up with the grim reality of the situation. He'd nearly lost control of himself, and now Antonia had fled.

It wasn't supposed to go this way. Yes, he'd intended a kiss, sweet and reverent. As one should, when one had enough experience to master his ardor and was trying to slowly coax desire from an innocent. Not like a starving man seated in front of a feast.

Stroking her tongue with his. Gripping the soft curve of her waist until her hips rolled against his erection. No wonder she'd pushed him back and run away. Yes, she'd responded eagerly to him, so eagerly that it had brought him to a fever pitch, but that didn't change the fact that he should have slowed the momentum. Had she been frightened of her own reaction? Or worse, frightened of him?

"Damn it to hell," he growled. He'd almost certainly ruined any chance he'd had with her. He dimly thought about the wager, but couldn't bring himself to care at the moment. All that mattered was making amends with Antonia.

His cock now reluctantly behaving, he pushed himself off the wall and sped downstairs. However, by the time he reached the parlor, she was nowhere to be found, and the rest of the guests had returned. Apparently, De Brienne had made no effort to best his lover, and Victoire had easily outscored him.

Things weren't any better that evening. Antonia finally appeared, stoking the hope that he might find a moment alone with her, apologize and prove to her that he could act like a perfect gentleman, although the way the snug bodice of her dress plumped up her bosom certainly wasn't helping.

It was all in vain, however. She barely glanced at him and remained at Claudine's side the entire night, carefully keeping herself at a distance. And again the next morning, when she disappeared with a group of matrons to visit the village market, and the afternoon, when she'd claimed a headache and stayed locked up in her room.

By the time the following evening came, Guy felt like a wild horse in a tight harness.

"A left hook, right hook, and then he turns and kicks his heel square into the other's jaw. I'm telling you, it was one of the most brutal fights I've ever seen."

Nicolas had been blathering on about a *savate* match since they'd left the billiards room with the vague intent of taking a turn around the card tables. He could've been speaking bloody English and Guy would have barely noticed the difference.

"Boutin is a future champion, mark my words, the man is built like an ox and quick as a cat. Though I managed to hold my own against him. Experience, I suppose, nothing like years in the streets to acquire technique. Wouldn't you agree? Guy?"

"How the hell should I know?" he snarled in response.

Nicolas burst out laughing and held up his arms in mock defense. "Easy, man. Whatever your problem is, I doubt it has anything to do with me."

Guy straightened his jacket and lowered his voice. "I don't have a problem."

"Indeed, I rather think you have several. And one of them is heading our way right now."

Victoire ambled toward them, dressed in a splendid silver creation that shimmered with every movement of her hips. "Monsieur de Cazal, I was wondering if I could ask your opinion on something. Books, to be exact."

"Such a monotonous subject coming from such a vivacious mouth," Nicolas said. "Pity. I'll leave you to it."

He watched Nicolas leave and sighed. "What is it, Victoire?"

She stretched her neck and fanned herself, bringing attention to her plunging neckline. "Oh, just trying to liven another long evening of card playing. Gambling does get a bit tiresome after a while, especially when the stakes are so low."

"And you're hoping to entertain yourself with a book?"

"Indeed. But the Aubertin's library holds so many volumes, I need someone to recommend something stimulating. Would you be kind enough to help me? It might distract you from your troubles and bring us both enjoyment."

Her meaning was crystal clear. The library was always deserted at this hour, with everyone busy playing cards and drinking. Guy had no doubt Victoire didn't intend to give herself completely to him, but perhaps she could lessen the ache. The faint stir of interest was like a distant echo of what he'd once coveted with such determination.

"At your service, *madame*."

A satisfied smile played on her rosy lips. "Meet me there in half an hour. Another glass of cognac or two and Xavier will be too foxed to pay attention."

He nodded and made his way straight to the library, glad to escape the din and agitation for one blessed moment. It was a large, handsome room, and François's collection of books was just as impressive as his cognac reserves and wine cellar: the volumes covered an entire wall from top to bottom. A single taper was lit on the small table between two large window nooks fitted with cushioned seats.

Guy walked over to the shelves and let his fingers brush slowly against the spines of the books, just as he did when he was a child. He'd always loved the smell of the weathered paper, the softness of the leather, the faint flap of the pages as he let them slide under his thumb. His father had often reprimanded him for his lack of interest in what they actually contained. Joseph de Cazal was a learned man, a disciple of the Enlightenment, and a firm believer in radical reforms that would lead to a society of equals.

In the end, his books and his ideals hadn't saved him. They hadn't saved anyone. Guy let his hand drop to his side and went to sit in one of the window seats, staring at the darkness outside.

Steps resonated in the corridor. Had Victoire already managed to get rid of Xavier? No, there were two people approaching. Another assignation, perhaps, he thought with a smirk.

"Trust me, no one will bother us in here."

He froze. Claudine. On instinct, he grabbed the velvet curtain hanging beside him and swept it over the nook, a second before she entered the room.

Antonia must be with her. It wasn't just a logical deduction. He could sense her presence with every nerve and every muscle in his body. He remained perfectly still, barely daring to take a breath. If there was any chance at all that he could gain insight on why Antonia was avoiding him, hiding was worth the risk.

"Now, my dear, you must tell me what is wrong. You seem… despondent. It is most unlike you."

"I'm sorry if I caused you any worry," came Antonia's soft, melodious voice. "It's nothing, really."

"Please forgive me if I'm too forward, but does it have anything to do with Monsieur de Cazal?"

A pause, then a little sigh he wished he could feel against his lips. "I've never been very good at concealing my feelings."

"You may not be entirely to blame. Marie-Louise always told me I'm extremely astute at reading people." Claudine laughed at her own words, eliciting a small chuckle from Antonia, then continued in a more subdued tone. "Though anyone with eyes can see that he shows a particular inclination toward you and may wish to follow up on your previous attachment. He's a scoundrel, to be sure, but he's cultivated and well-spoken, not to mention ridiculously handsome. Is there any particular reason why you shouldn't return his favor?"

A longer silence this time.

"Unless he has acted in an indelicate manner?"

Guy bit down on his lip. Was Antonia going to tell her about their kiss? After all, it had been far from delicate.

"I suppose you could say so… but it happened a long time ago, when we were much younger, and he didn't know he had offended me. In fact he still doesn't know."

She stopped. Most likely hesitant to continue. He gripped the velvet cushioning. By God, he would go crazy if he didn't find out what on earth she was talking about.

"You can confide in me, my dear," Claudine encouraged her. "I know I appear to be a dreadful busybody, and I may say a great many silly things when I've a bit too much to drink, but never have I betrayed the trust of a friend."

Antonia took a deep breath. "It was a few weeks before my parents died, before the Terror forced us to leave. The last time we were all together, as a matter of fact. We had been invited by the de Cazals for dinner. I knew it was our parents' dearest wish that Guy and I become betrothed, but I wasn't expecting them to make an announcement that very evening. I was only fourteen, and it would be years until we could marry."

He winced silently, cold dread dropping like a lead brick in his stomach. He didn't want to hear the rest. He didn't want to think about his family home, or the dinners his parents hosted there, or Antonia when she was still Toinette. The urge to reveal his presence and bolt from the library was only overpowered by his knowledge that it would make matters far worse.

"Were you unhappy with the prospect?"

"Quite the contrary. I couldn't imagine marrying anyone else. I was besotted with him, as only a young, inexperienced girl can be. When they raised their glasses to us, I was embarrassed with the attention, but I desperately wanted it to come true."

His face burned with shame. He remembered that evening quite well, though he'd done his damnedest to forget it: his annoyance at his father's ceremonial words and his mother's tearful gaze, his boredom, his desire to be elsewhere. He hadn't given a single thought as to what Antonia might have felt.

"And him?"

"He just smiled politely and drank his wine. But later that evening, I was wandering in the gardens, looking at the full moon. Marguerite—Guy's mother—grew the loveliest roses in all of Chartres. I thought it was all terribly romantic, foolish thing that I was."

His heart splintered in his chest. His mother. That blasted, beautiful rose garden. How much more of this could he bear? No matter. He owed it to Antonia to listen until the end.

"Aren't we all foolish at that age? Please, go on."

"I heard some noises coming from the gazebo, so I tiptoed closer. It was Guy and the groundskeeper's daughter, Aurélie. They didn't see me, they were too busy kissing and whispering to each other… She teased him about his betrothal, and he said that it was all a farce, that he would never marry someone like me, and both of them mocked me quite cruelly."

He was dumbfounded. He had no recollection of the episode in the gazebo, and only vague images of Aurélie. A wide sultry smile, dark hair... Her face blurred with those of other dark-haired women he had known. How could Antonia remember so clearly something he had no memory of?

He closed his eyes and gave in to the bitter truth. She'd been enamored with him, that was why. Something he'd suspected at the time but brushed off as easily and callously as an insect on his sleeve.

"Maybe I shouldn't hold this against him," Antonia concluded, her voice wavering. "It was so long ago, but..."

"Some wounds take a long time to heal, if they heal at all." Claudine's tone was wistful, almost sad, but it quickly regained its usual cheer. "There, there, dry your tears, my dear. Monsieur de Cazal isn't the only eligible gentleman in France, is he? I have an idea that might lift your spirits."

That, at least, brought him back to the present, but it provided no relief. Whatever Claudine had in mind, it was sure to put another wrench in his plans.

Chapter Six

"I MUST SAY, I thought you a most pugnacious sort, *monsieur*."

Guy glanced up from the book he had been trying to read for the last half hour. Victoire was leaning against the stone balustrade of the terrace, the elegant slope of her neck emphasized by a flowing pink gown that revealed a good portion of her shoulders.

He returned to his book. "And to what do I owe this remark?"

She gave a little laugh, took the *Essay on Revolutions* from him and snapped it shut. "Will you not take a turn around the pond with me?"

Guy rose, retrieved the volume, and set it down on his chair; Chateaubriand deserved more attention than his troubled mind could give him at present. "As you wish. Just as long as you don't take your parasol."

Victoire raised an eyebrow. "How very respectable of you. Has the heat sapped your virility? That would explain a great many things. For example, why you left the library in such a dreadful hurry the other night."

She took his arm and, together, they descended the stone steps to the gardens. Thankfully, as the day was cooling, there were other people on the terrace. He'd be damned if he let himself go anywhere with Victoire where they weren't in plain sight, lest she think he wanted to remedy their failed assignation in the library. As soon as Claudine and Antonia had left, he'd remained seated at the window, trying desperately to gather his wits. When Victoire had arrived, he'd made up a paltry excuse, something about a sudden headache, and retreated to his room.

In fact, his virility was fine. More than fine. Raging, to the point where sleep eluded him and rest was impossible. He got up at the crack of dawn to ride, pushing his mount as hard as he dared, relishing in the thundering of the hooves as the sun rose on the countryside. He took part in any and all activity that was suggested. He drank wine and cognac and talked with Nicolas well into the night. He'd even taken to sampling what François's library had to offer. He'd exhausted himself—to no avail. This agony had gone on for two days and he was at his wits' end.

But he wasn't about to explain this to Victoire. It had nothing to do with her.

He shot her a sideways look as they strolled over to the pond. She was as stunning as ever in her rose-colored dress, the picture of flawless allure and radiant charm. He had recognized it immediately when they met. He recognized it still. So why did it have no more effect on him now than looking at an ornate vase of fine porcelain sitting on a shelf?

"Mademoiselle Saint Yves has been avoiding you since the archery tournament," Victoire remarked. "A rather surprising turn of events, given that she let you put your hands all over her. What did you do to scare off the little mouse?"

He gave a weary sigh. "I don't wish to discuss this with you."

"Fine. I take it you don't know yourself. In any case, I am more curious as to why *you*'ve given up on trying to pursue her. You've been avoiding her just as much."

"I haven't given anything up," he replied tersely.

In truth, his mind was in a tumult. Kissing Antonia had been like opening a floodgate of desire that threatened to drown him if he let his guard down. The feel of her soft lips against his, first hesitant, then eagerly pliant to his demands, her small hands gripping his shirt, the instinctive flow of her body against his, and the sweet, intoxicating fragrance of honeysuckle—it was all he could think about. One perfect moment, but it hadn't been enough. It was nowhere near enough.

Yet misfortune had brought him to overhear her conversation with Claudine, and he simply couldn't forget what she'd explained with excruciating candor. No wonder Antonia had regarded him so coldly at first. If she'd spent her years in exile brooding over the last memory she had of him, his heartless words and the kisses he'd shared with another, it was a miracle she even spoke to him, and a testament to her gentle nature than she had offered him her friendship.

What a complete and utter ass he'd been. And would continue to be, if he kept this up. He simply couldn't go through with this wager. But staying away from her, now that he had tasted the exquisite pleasures he was depriving himself of, was torment.

"Am I to conclude that our wager still stands?" Victoire pressed him.

Her honeyed voice hid an edge of imperiousness. He recognized it well. She ordered De Brienne about with the same tone. And now she wanted to hear Guy reaffirm that he would do anything to be her lover, or that he couldn't possibly seduce Antonia when he was already devoted to a woman of superior beauty and character.

He was in no mood to indulge her, but neither did he want to tell her outright that the wager was off. Victoire was no fool, and God only knew what she would do if she found out his attentions were now focused on Antonia alone. He'd already witnessed her cutting through the armor of other women, women of the Parisian *beau monde* with wealth and connections, just to find their weak spot and humiliate them publicly, because they had displeased her in one way or another.

Victoire was a huntress. He used to think they were much the same. Now all he wanted to do was protect Antonia from her verbal darts.

He gave her a cool smile. "There's been a temporary setback due to unexpected circumstances, that is all. If I did not adapt my strategy, I would be a paltry seducer indeed."

"Good. If there's one thing I hate even more than losing, it's not playing at all."

They had arrived halfway around the pond and Guy, momentarily nonplussed by Victoire's tart reply, spotted two riders on top of the slope leading to the chateau. When they trotted closer, he realized the two young men were strangers to the party.

"What now?" he muttered.

His answer came in the form of an enthusiastic cheer. Claudine and Antonia had come out on to the terrace, and the older woman raised both arms in the air to wave at the riders.

"Baptiste!" she called out. "Over here, my darling boy!"

My darling boy? Guy squinted at the newcomers. "Is that…?"

"Madame Rouget's son?" Victoire completed with a sly grin. "Yes, I might have heard her ask Marie-Louise if she could invite him for a visit. And look, he brought a friend! One can never have too many available gentlemen at a house party."

So this was Claudine's plan to lift Antonia's spirits. Damn her. The woman fancied herself a matchmaker.

The riders halted their mounts a few meters from the terrace, and Claudine hurried down the stone steps to greet them, with Antonia trailing behind her.

Guy quickly calculated his options. He could continue on the same path and return to the chateau, which would lead them straight to where Claudine and Antonia were now standing, which would *then* lead to introductions and possibly having to stand there like a fool while Claudine started her idiotic campaign to make Antonia her daughter-in-law. Or he could take another turn around the basin with Victoire and draw out an already unpleasant conversation. A fine choice between cholera and the plague.

With a weary sigh, he pressed Victoire forward to the chateau. If the riders were tired from their journey, there was a chance this wouldn't last too long, and he couldn't deny a certain begrudging curiosity at how Antonia would react to Claudine's machinations.

"… found the road rather pleasant," Guy heard Rouget say when they arrived within earshot of the group. "Wasn't much trouble at all to come from Civry. The carriage is only a short way behind us."

"I'm ever so glad you've arrived safely," Claudine replied. "Oh, silly me, I haven't introduced you! This is Antonia Saint Yves, the young lady I was telling you about in my letter. Antonia, my beloved son, Baptiste."

Good God, she wasn't wasting any time, was she? The young man tipped his hat. "A pleasure, *mademoiselle*."

Guy was now close enough to make out his features: plump and ruddy-cheeked, with an affable expression not unlike his mother's. Antonia dropped into a short, graceful curtsy.

Rouget turned to his companion. "And this is my friend, Monsieur Jacques Lenoir. We met in Paris a few months ago."

Lenoir tipped his hat as well but remained silent. Guy frowned. Something about that man's demeanor… He was dressed in an ordinary riding outfit, but the way he held himself on the saddle was uneasy, and his poor horse foamed at the mouth from gnawing at his bit and straining against excessively tight reins. In Guy's experience, a man who took out his emotions on his mount was not to be trusted.

"Rather handsome, that one," Victoire remarked as if she were appraising a prize stud instead of a man. "Too bad *he's* not her son, or they would publish the banns within a week."

"Oh, and what luck!" Claudine exclaimed. "Here come Monsieur de Cazal and Madame Le Plessis Tailland."

Antonia met Guy's gaze and that beautiful flush he took so much pleasure in eliciting appeared on her cheeks. His chest rumbled with satisfaction. Rouget certainly hadn't made her blush that way.

A fresh round of introductions was made, after which Claudine regaled them with an account of her son's successful training in a prestigious notary cabinet in Paris. Rouget was starting to shift uncomfortably atop his horse.

"*Maman*, perhaps this can wait until later," he said. "Our horses need rest, and we need a bath and a change of clothes."

"Yes, of course. You go right along, my darling, and we'll be waiting for you with refreshments."

Rouget nodded and led his horse away. Lenoir still hadn't said a word and followed him like a shadow. Unsettling fellow.

As if he needed further proof to confirm his instinct, Guy spotted Nicolas standing at the window from inside the chateau, staring down at them. That, too, was bizarre. His friend usually delighted in making new acquaintances, and he certainly wouldn't pass up the chance to see Guy flounder for polite conversation between Antonia and Victoire.

His own problems momentarily slipped from his mind, and he excused himself, leaving the ladies at the foot of the stone steps to return inside.

He found Nicolas in the same spot: at the window of the empty billiards room, clasping his hands behind his back.

"What's the matter?" Guy asked, placing a hand on his shoulder. "That man accompanying Claudine's son... Lenoir. Do you know him?"

"I did," Nicolas said shortly.

His expression had hardened into a sharp awareness that suddenly reminded Guy of where his friend had come from, and what he had done to survive. It was easy to forget, so carefully hidden behind the witty quips and foppish clothes.

"What about him, then?" he asked.

Nicolas turned away from the window. "Trouble."

"Saint Emilion La Tour du Pin. Ha! A rather bold choice with duck *aiguillettes*. I think I would've gone with a Médoc."

Baptiste swirled his wine glass in his hand, then took another gulp, carefully savoring the taste. Antonia took a bite of the delicious, tender duck strips which had been served with a honeyed sauce and managed a smile. It was hard to properly enjoy such an excellent meal when two blue eyes were boring through her from the other side of the table.

Claudine had loudly insisted that Antonia be seated between her and Baptiste and would not let the conversation between them lull even for a second. She seemed determined, in her own ruthlessly jolly manner, for Antonia to find out as much as possible about her son in the space of one evening, as if she was hoping for an engagement before luncheon tomorrow.

And indeed, it didn't take much time at all to determine what sort of man Baptiste was. Sociable, well-mannered, unpretentious. He liked horses, the law, and fine dining. His company was perfectly pleasant.

Pleasant, yes. Not the type to make a woman shift uncomfortably in her chair by staring at her with a burning gaze.

"What do you think, Mademoiselle Saint Yves?"

"I'm afraid I'm unlearned in wine pairings," she replied, forcing herself to look at Baptiste and not, under any circumstance, left and across from her seat. "Ten years in London certainly didn't help in that regard. My brother and brother-in-law often complained that there wasn't a single drop of proper wine to be found in England, though they developed quite a taste for ale."

"It's never too late to start your education, my dear," Claudine said. "The man of the house must maintain a proper wine cellar, but then it's the duty of the hostess to come up with dishes to go with it. Once you're married, that will fall to you."

It was touching, really, that Claudine thought so highly of her that she was pushing her toward Baptiste with such fervor. Yet the constant barrage of good will and thinly veiled allusions was starting to deplete Antonia's vast reserves of patience.

Cutting into another piece of duck, she dared a glance across the table. Guy was busy talking to Nicolas, who appeared to be lacking his usual vivacity.

"Well, Lenoir and I attended a party last month, not far from the Tuileries, where the wine was the best I've ever tasted. Lalande Pomerol, if I'm not mistaken. Excellent vintage."

"Speaking of which, why did Monsieur Lenoir not join us for dinner? I must tell you, Marie-Louise was a bit vexed and I even more so, as the proportion of gentlemen to ladies still weighs in our favor."

Baptiste gulped down his food, looking like a child who had been caught doing something naughty. "He was feeling tired from our travels. We had to get up very early this morning and…"

Claudine let her hands drop on both sides of her place and raised her eyes to the heavens. "Am I to understand that you spent the entire night merry-making, *again*?"

"*Maman*, please, we were just playing cards, and then Pierrot absolutely insisted on reading to us the play he'd been working on. You know how he is when he's in his cups…"

As Claudine and Baptiste went on gabbling, Antonia looked at Guy again. This time, their gazes met head on. Her breath hitched in her chest. His eyes were a swirl of hot anger and steady determination. It didn't bear thinking what he was so determined to do, not if she wanted to keep her composure until supper was over. The unbearable weight of his scrutiny, as if Guy was ready to pummel Baptiste every time he addressed her, made her feel singled out. Desired. Claimed.

Guy briefly turned away and took a sip of wine, his tongue flicking out to run between his lips. A pool of heat gathered within her, low and deep, impervious to the way she squeezed her legs together to dissipate it.

She gripped her napkin between her fingers, alarmed at the ease with which he tore down her defenses. After their kiss, she'd done her best to avoid him. Hurt, confusion, yearning, all of it made it impossible to think clearly, and she needed to find her rational footing again. Confessing to Claudine what had been weighing on her all these years had helped. However, to her surprise, Guy hadn't sought her out to demand an explanation. In fact, he'd spent most of his time outdoors and had taken part in any and all activities that their hosts organized, impeding any chance for them to be alone. She'd tampered her disappointment by trying to convince herself that it was for the best.

But after Baptiste's arrival, in the space of a few hours, the intensity of Guy's jealous attention had made her resolve melt like ice in the midday sun.

"Oh look, they're about to serve the *entremets*. Strawberry mousse, is it? It will do very well before the cheese plate."

Antonia retreated back into the safety of the Rougets' chatter. If the *entremets* were being served, dinner would soon be over.

However, her hopes of making a quick escape to her room were dashed when Claudine insisted she join in a few rounds of pinochle so that Baptiste could give her some pointers, as it was his favorite card game. After two hands, Claudine's eyelids began to droop, and Baptiste suggested they take a turn around the terrace.

"Forgive me," Antonia said, hiding a fake yawn behind her hand. "I am quite tired myself. Perhaps it's best if I…"

"Come now, a bit of fresh air will restore your spirits. After our fete last evening, I'm surprised I haven't fallen asleep at the dinner table, but I suppose riding all day did the trick. Isn't that funny!"

Once they were outside, Baptiste leaned on the stone balustrade and breathed in deeply, then turned back to her. "I meant to thank you for your kind friendship toward my mother."

"It is I who should thank her," Antonia replied. "I did nothing but respond to her generosity."

"Generous, yes, to the point of being overbearing at times. And she has never terribly minded her manners either."

He was much the same, talking about his own mother in this fashion. Speaking whatever came through one's mind must be a family trait. But Antonia maintained a polite smile. Baptiste didn't mean anything hurtful by it. He was simply… young. Young and buoyant and untried by life, though they were close in age. True, his father had died, but Claudine had mentioned weak lungs, a hunting session in January and a bad case of pneumonia. Antonia knew only too well the pain of losing a parent to illness, yet such tragedies were commonplace.

How had the Rougets managed to pass through the Terror relatively unscathed? How had anyone managed? Connections? A protector? Sheer luck? Such twists of fate seemed as random as the roll of a dice.

"I must admit, I was surprised she invited me here. Whenever the Aubertins come to visit, she and Marie-Louise spend their time chatting like schoolgirls and I'm told to run along whenever I try to join in the conversation." His rosy cheeks turned crimson. "But I do see why she was so intent on introducing you to me."

"I'd say introductions have been made now, haven't they?"

Antonia's heart leaped in her chest. Guy had stepped out onto the terrace and was advancing toward them like a predator getting ready for the kill.

"Monsieur de Cazal," Baptiste greeted him with oblivious cheer. "So nice of you to join us."

Nice was the last adjective Antonia would have applied to the situation. She looked at Guy, silently pleading him not to make a scene, but he kept his focus on Baptiste.

"I was searching for Mademoiselle Saint Yves," he said. "Imagine my surprise when I found her out here with you."

"Just a natural continuation of our conversation at the dinner table," Baptiste replied. "Most invigorating to enjoy a bit of coolness after such a hot day, isn't it?"

Guy looked down his nose at him, with all the assurance and disdain his broader frame allowed him. "Some might say a dutiful son would stay with his mother and make sure she's not losing too much at the card table, instead of worrying about his *vigor*."

Baptiste's gaze flickered toward Claudine, who was dozing

softly in her chair, and he swallowed audibly, realization dawning on his face. "You're quite right. I shall return inside."

Once they were alone, Antonia turned to Guy, her face tight with annoyance. At least he had the decency not to look smug. "That was very impolite of you. Clearly Claudine doesn't need her son's assistance at present. Do you think him a fool? What right did you have to interrupt our discussion?"

"Forgive me if I deprived you of Rouget's scintillating presence," he replied shortly. "I need to talk to you."

"It doesn't appear to me that you're in any mood to talk."

He pressed his lips together and hesitated before answering. "And yet it must be done."

She crossed her arms in front of her chest. "Why now? After you've been avoiding me for days?"

He looked down at his feet for a moment, then back at her, his blue eyes filled with something close to anguish. "You seemed upset. I didn't know the best way to go about it."

"So you simply barged in while I was trying to get to know Monsieur Rouget better."

The burning anger returned. "As a matter of courtesy, or as a prospective husband? If it's the latter you're being remarkably efficient."

The words stung her like a slap. "How dare you?" she hissed. "And why would *you* even care one way or the other?"

She couldn't stand being in his presence a moment longer. It was too overwhelming, too painful. She turned on her heel and started down the steps of the terrace, out into the beckoning darkness, where she might find peace and quiet at last.

Guy caught up with her just as she had reached the graveled path. "Antonia, wait. Wait."

He grabbed her wrist and she whipped around to face him.

"I'm sorry, that was unspeakably rude," he said, more softly. "And it's not the only thing I have to apologize for. What happened between us the other day…"

The kiss. Of course. She should have known from the way he

had avoided her that he was wary of her reading too much into it. "What about it?"

He cleared his throat and delivered his line as if he had practiced it many times beforehand. "It was wrong of me to behave like that toward you. I took advantage of the situation in a most brutish manner. It won't happen again."

Her stomach plummeted to her feet. "I see. You regret that we kissed."

"No," he retorted immediately. "I... I regret that I let it go that far."

That did it. First Claudine trying to push her toward Baptiste, now Guy speaking as if she had been a passive participant in their kiss, all of them treating her like a rag doll to be tossed around. Just like she'd been tossed around for years, going from one place to the next with no say in the matter, dutifully letting others determine what she should or shouldn't do.

"Explain to me why you should take the blame for something we both did," she snapped. "I didn't protest, or cower, or ask you to stop. In fact, I remember responding with... enthusiasm."

And it was all too easy to remember where that particular sort of enthusiasm came from, when he was so near, though perhaps it wasn't the right word. Many would call in wantonness, and certainly what she'd always been taught was that unmarried women were under no circumstances to give in to that particular weakness.

Yet it hadn't felt like a weakness. It had felt like a revelation, like uncovering a side of herself she hadn't known existed. A side that scared her and thrilled her at the same time.

A muscle ticked in Guy's jaw. He clasped his hands behind his back. "That's beside the point."

"Well, I fail to see what the point *is*, if not denying my capacity to decide on my own." The crack in her composure was rapidly fanning out, and all the resentment that had lain dormant for so long now flowed free. "I may not be experienced and worldly like Madame Le Plessis or any of the other Parisian coquettes you've been with, but neither I am a featherbrained ingenue. I know myself. And now, I know my own desire."

He greeted the onslaught of her words with utter silence and an unreadable expression. As the seconds ticked by, she resisted the growing urge to flee and lock herself in her room and never face him again. Finally, he casually smoothed the lapels of his coat and straightened his cuffs, even as his gaze pinned her down with devastating intensity.

"Do you? Do you really?" he rasped. "Tell me then, Antonia, in the simplest terms. What is it you desire?"

Chapter Seven

D EVIL TAKE IT. This hell of an evening might yet be salvaged.
Guy had tried to do the honorable thing. Tried to warn
her off. Tried to keep his temper in check, even after a five-course
dinner where he watched Rouget's inept attempts at conversation
monopolize her by force of politeness, until his hands were
itching to throttle the damn fool. With Nicolas sullen at his side,
evading his questions and emptying his wine glass as quickly as
possible without passing for a drunkard, there was no one,
nothing to distract Guy from the gnawing urge to lay claim to
Antonia's attentions.

Still, he'd done what he must. He'd apologized, and even as
his lust fought tooth and nail not to be denied, he'd meant to
keep his promise.

But Antonia was having none of it, flinging his apology in his
face and daring him to reply to her assertion. *I know my own desire.*
So be it, then. He was never one to back down when a gauntlet
was thrown. Especially not by a delicate, fine hand he fantasized
seeing wrapped around his cock.

Now, though, her bold words had evaporated, leaving only
nervousness. Even if her natural reserve hid a wellspring of
passion, no one had ever taught her how to speak of it, leaving
him to voice what they both wanted.

He straightened his shoulders and stepped closer.

"I see you're having some trouble putting it into words. Let me help you. Perhaps you simply fancy another kiss?"

Her lips parted slightly but she didn't reply. He took her hand, then led her a few steps into one of the sculpted alcoves under the balustrade. Sheltered from the light of the lamps, hidden from view, the alcove seemed almost intimate. And they would need all the intimacy they could get for what he had in mind.

But first things first. He pressed his mouth tenderly on hers, breaking away after only a second.

"There. Is that enough to satisfy you?"

In her gray eyes, confusion was fighting a losing battle against lust. "Guy... I—I don't..."

He placed his finger under the tip of her chin, lifted it, and took her mouth again. Deeper this time, nipping at her bottom lip, opening her mouth to his tongue's caress. His hands fell to her waist and he pulled her closer, but not close enough that she would feel his growing arousal.

"Better?" he murmured.

She gave a small nod, her gaze hooded, her bosom straining against the neckline of her bodice. It was too dim for him to see if her skin was flushed, but the heat radiating from her and the way her body was swaying toward his, like a moth irresistibly fluttering toward a flame, was more than enough to go by.

He kneaded the soft flesh of her hips under the delicate cloth of her dress. "I can stop here. Unless there is something else that you want?"

Her eyes squeezed shut for a moment, as if she was trying to gain a hold of herself. Oh, how he craved for that hold to slip entirely, for her ardor to rise and sweep over her. But he didn't press her. Didn't need to. She swallowed, her voice a thin thread of yearning. "Yes."

Innocent beauty. Teaching her the language of lust was a pleasure almost as acute as the act itself.

"Would you like me to put my hands on you?" he rumbled. "Is that it? All you have to do is ask. I can feel your eagerness, just there, on the surface of your skin."

He traced the tip of his forefinger up her arm, then let it stray on the side of her neck, her collarbone, the smooth plane leading between her breasts. "Speak it, love, so I can give you what you need."

"Touch me," she whispered at last. "*Please*, touch me."

"Where should I touch you?" She arched forward in a wordless plea and his palm cupped her breast. "Right there?"

For a moment he simply marveled in the weight and feel of her, how perfectly she fit in his hand, the lovely sigh escaping from her throat as he squeezed the plump curve. But it wasn't enough. The soft material of her dress couldn't possibly compare to what lay under it.

He deftly inched his fingers down her bodice until he finally coaxed out the puckered bud of her breast, grazing it with the pad of his thumb, eliciting a soft moan.

"So sensitive. Responding to the merest brush. If I were to put my mouth here—" He lightly pinched the dusky tip. "—do you suppose it would give you pleasure?"

She nodded frantically. He drew his hand away, drunk on the need to hear her voice, the hushed words spilling from her lips as she gave in completely to her passion.

"Answer me," he demanded. "I won't do anything until I'm certain it's what you want."

A boldfaced lie. A team of raring horses couldn't stop him now. His hunger for her was too great, too intense, barely controllable.

"*Yes*," she whimpered. "It would… give me great pleasure."

He tugged her bodice down, baring her full breasts. His mouth descended along her neck until it reached the sensitive, puckered tip aching to be licked and sucked.

Antonia threw her head back against the stone wall as he lavished her nipples with his tongue, one after the other, teasing them into taut points, until her harsh breaths mirrored his own.

Finally, he released the sweet, engorged crest and raised his head again to look at her. She was panting, writhing against him, her hips now aligned with his straining erection.

"I am at your service, Antonia. There's nothing you could ask of me now that I wouldn't do to satiate you. Tell me, do you know what happens when a woman reaches her peak?"

"Something… about a great and painful pressure being appeased, but…"

She shook her head, struggling to remember words she had heard long ago, no doubt from more experienced women, who implied many things but explained little. No matter. Soon she would understand for herself. That he would be the first to bring her such sweet release sent a heated thrill through him unlike any he had ever known.

"And do you know how to reach that peak?"

His right hand traveled down to her thigh. He bunched the soft material of her dress until his fingers brushed the hem and, underneath, silken softness.

"No. No, I…"

"But you feel where the ache is deepest, don't you?" His own voice was thick with lust, almost desperate. He needed to feel her against his fingers, needed to delve into the tight lushness until she came apart. "Show me. Guide my hand."

She placed her small hand over his, slowly dragging it over her thighs to her supple folds. Slick and ready to open for him. He groaned. By God, it was all he could not to tear at his breeches and drive into her.

"That's right. Just there." He pressed his palm where the throb was most acute, stroking the length of her with his middle finger. "Do you feel how wet you are?"

She swallowed and nodded, and a sliver of embarrassment passed over her features.

"No, none of that," he told her sharply. "It is your body's way of saying what it craves. A gift that will bring us both indescribable pleasure." He pressed his finger against the entrance of her sheath. "Is this what you want? Tell me."

She was so close already, a hairbreadth away from her climax, and her forehead dropped to his shoulder, hiding her face in a veil of titian curls.

"Guy," she moaned. "It's too much…"

"*Tell me*," he commanded.

"Yes. *Yes*. I… I want this. You. I want you."

He thrust his finger inside of her. "*That* is your desire, love." He pulled back and thrust again. "*That* is what you need." Again. "*That* is how you reach your peak."

Again, and again, and again. She muffled her cries against his jacket, rolling her hips to meet his hand, taking him in her tight, luscious heat until it pulsed and clenched. When exquisite quivers of her release slowed, he held her against his chest, her body limp and warm and perfectly cradled in his arms.

More, a voice in his mind urged him. *More. This isn't enough. This will never be enough.*

His arousal was still iron-hard, begging for its own release, but deep down inside, something else wavered. With each of Antonia's heartbeats, thumping so close to his, life was seeping back into him, ebullient and fruitful, full of color and beauty.

And when she gently untangled herself from him, her breathing restored, he saw it in her eyes: it would take next to nothing—perhaps but a single word—to make her his entirely, to gorge himself on the bliss that her body could offer.

More, the voice insisted. *Now.*

With any other woman, he would have given in to his urge in a second, without a care for propriety or consequences. He had lost every illusion he once had about respectable conduct long ago; what was the point of upholding morality when society could descend, almost overnight, into barbarity and bloodshed?

But Antonia… So gentle, so trusting, even after everything she'd been through… How could he bed her and conceal his initial deception? What if she found out afterwards? Given the chance, Victoire would tell her. Antonia would be devastated. Again. By his fault.

He must speak up now, before he caused irreparable damage. He must, though he knew she would no longer want anything to do with him.

"Damnation," he growled, stroking her mussed curls, caught in a trap of his own making, thrashing helplessly against the steel jaws of his desire. "This is unbearable."

She put her bodice back into place and frowned. "What's wrong?"

He stepped away from her, raking his hands through his hair. As if it could help sort the whirlwind in his mind. There was only one way to make it stop.

"I want you, Antonia. Never doubt that I want you. So much I have scarcely been able to think of anything else since you arrived. Even when we are apart, it drives me to distraction."

She inhaled sharply and opened her mouth. He held his hand and shook his head. If she told him she felt the same, he would be done for.

"Before coming to Verneuil, Victoire and I..." The words weighed in his chest like a ton of lead. In a second, they would crush Antonia as well. By God, how could he live with himself after this? "We'd been discussing a possible arrangement, such as is possible with a married woman. As a final condition to her favor, she dared me to prove my skills as a lover by seducing you during the party."

And she was also making sure he had no attachment to Antonia whatsoever, in spite of their betrothal. But he couldn't speak that part out loud. Couldn't even contemplate his own feelings on the matter. Like a pool both brilliant and black, swirling deep within his heart, they threatened to drown him. Watching Antonia's face losing its glow of ecstasy and take on a ghastly pallor was torturous enough.

"And you accepted?" she asked quietly.

He forced himself not to look away. "I did."

Antonia said nothing. Looked down. Smoothed her rumpled dress. "Will this suffice?"

A dagger twisting into his gut couldn't possibly be more painful than this. He tried to grab her hand but she lurched back, her eyes blazing and her mouth set in a grim line.

"Antonia, I… The wager was a cruel, obscene ploy. It fled my mind as soon as I saw you, and I no longer cared about any of it. What just happened… it had nothing to do with it, I swear. Please believe me."

"No. I will not. Claudine was wrong about you." She lifted her chin even as the tears started to well and drove the dagger in deeper. "You are well and truly a *débauché.*"

She turned away and fled, leaving the word hanging in the air, and him alone in the dark with his misery.

"WHAT DO YOU think of this one, *mademoiselle*? It would complement your blue gown well."

Antonia pretended to be interested in the length of silver cord Lisette was presenting to her. Ever since she had taken note of the Grecian hairstyles mastered by the Parisian maids, Lisette had been determined to try her hand on her mistress whose hair, she claimed, had the perfect amount of curl and thickness for it.

"Yes, that'll be lovely," Antonia replied, forcing her mouth into a slight smile and taking a few coins out of her reticule to hand them to her. "Buy as much as you need."

"Hmmm. Might as well pick up something for myself while we're here. I always wear red on the Feast of Saint John and I could use some new hair ribbons."

Lisette's voice was giddy with excitement. Tonight, all over the countryside, bonfires would blaze, music would fill the air, and everyone, from the loftiest lord to the lowliest servant, would spend the short hours of the night dancing and carousing. The entire village of Verneuil buzzed with activity in preparation for the event.

Antonia, meanwhile, had never felt so wretched.

A day and a half had passed since… She didn't know exactly what to call it. An assignation? A tryst? Rather a moment of pure, unfettered ecstasy followed by a brutal descent into the harshness of reality. But there was no word for that.

Neither was there a proper word for what she was feeling. She wanted to hate Guy, write him off as a blackguard once and for all. And she was still angry at him—furious, in fact, to the point where it burned and crackled over her skin whenever she thought back on what he'd told her. Let him keep his stupid wager with that brazen harpy. Let him swallow back his own shame until it he choked on it.

But her heart was too tender to scorn and dismiss entirely. And her body—oh, her body was much too slow to forget.

Guy had kept his distance. He hadn't tried to intimidate Baptiste, or barge into a conversation, or find himself alone with her to apologize again. But once in a while, she felt his eyes on her, lingering, longing, heavy with regret. Regret and something else.

Desire. Blasted, cursed, inescapable desire.

She couldn't fight it. Neither his nor her own. Last night, she had dreamed of him, how his hard, muscled weight would feel on top of her, how his strong hands would grip every soft part of her body, how his skilled tongue would set off spirals of pleasure on her neck, her breasts. What if he kissed her elsewhere? Her entire body had burned at the idea. What if he let his lips stray down her stomach, and then reach the hidden spot where the need was most pressing? As soon as the wicked image materialized in her head, she shook it away. No. Impossible. This went far beyond what she dared imagine.

It had taken her a long time afterward to fall asleep.

Antonia stood in front of the row of colorful spools, staring blindly at them, wondering if she was going mad. The only true comfort had come yesterday in the form of a letter from

Honorine. It warmed Antonia's heart to read about the usual routine of their home, the antics of the children, her sister's mundane complaints and small delights—like running her hand over a well-loved embroidery.

However, it had also reminded her of Honorine's hopes for her: making connections, possibly a match. She had been so shaken by Guy's presence, so swept up by the feelings he elicited in her, like water reviving a withered flower, that she had forgotten that the rest of the world hadn't stopped turning. If she wanted a family of her own, she must marry, it was as simple as that.

And for all intents and purposes, Baptiste Rouget was suitable. He was a good-humored gentleman from a respectable family, and Antonia would be hard-pressed to find a friendlier, more accommodating mother-in-law than Claudine. She couldn't hold his lack of brooding blue gaze against him, nor the fact that she didn't feel that strange, heady tug between her thighs every time their eyes met.

The only thing one might begrudge him was his choice of friends. Jacques Lenoir was an odd sort, a taciturn man who kept to himself most of the time, though he was curtly polite when spoken to. And she supposed he was handsome enough, with his chestnut hair swept over his forehead and his dark brow. Yet something about his eyes unsettled her. They were always darting to and fro, weasel-like, as if he suspected danger might arise out of nowhere.

Baptiste seemed to admire him for his intimate knowledge of the capital, though this proved of little use here. Claudine, however, was not easily impressed. Her manner, though polite, lacked its usual warmth when addressing him, and she arranged whenever possible for Baptiste to be on his own with Antonia and herself.

Antonia fiddled with the edge of a lace ribbon and sighed. Probably just as much a scheme to further their connection as anything else. Baptiste didn't seem to mind his mother's meddling. Was he simply used to it, or would he respond favorably if Antonia encouraged him? There wasn't much time left to decide. The Aubertins had organized a ball overmorrow to mark the end of the festivities, and then she would leave, with or without a prospective betrothal.

Her throat tightened. For one wild moment, she imagined how easy everything would be, how thrilling and splendid it would feel, if only the man she had *already* been betrothed to held her in the same regard as she held him.

She let the ribbon drop. Suddenly, the stuffy, overcrowded shop pressed on her. Air. She needed air. She went to find Lisette.

"I'm going to take a walk around the village," she told her.

"Are you all right, *mademoiselle*?" the maid asked with concern.

"I'm fine, don't worry. It's just awfully hot in here. Take your time and wait for me outside the shop when you're done."

"As you wish, *mademoiselle*."

Antonia rushed outside. The street was almost as crowded as the shop, bustling with laborers, tradesmen and women carrying loaded baskets. She made her way down the cobbled pathway, hoping for a quieter place in which she could gather her thoughts. Her steps led her to the village church, a modest but sturdy edifice which sat on a stretch of lush grass. Under the timbered porch, a gaggle of children were busy making flower garlands to be hung on the pews in celebration of midsummer, but the rest of the area was deserted. Antonia smiled and drifted slowly across the grass, seeking the shade of the nearby birch trees.

She had almost made her way down the side of the edifice when she heard voices coming from an open portico in the back. Masculine voices, apparently in a heated argument, though they kept their tone low. And something about them struck her as familiar. She slowed her pace and kept close to the wall, approaching with caution.

"… no way to treat an old friend."

"*An old friend*? Am I to believe you're blackmailing me in the name of *friendship*?"

She covered her mouth to stifle a gasp. No wonder they struck her as familiar. Nicolas and Jacques Lenoir. What were they doing here? And what could they be arguing about with such acrimony? They had given no sign of even knowing each other.

"You weren't so high and mighty a few years back, Lefevre," Lenoir snickered. "You did far worse to lay your hands on some francs when your purse was empty."

"I'm not denying it," Nicolas bit back. "Doesn't make you less rotten, though."

"My funds are low. Leeching off Rouget hasn't been nearly as profitable as I hoped."

Antonia's eyes widened. *Leeching*? Claudine had seen right through him, then.

Nicolas gave a rough laugh. "Never one to mince words, eh? That's always been your problem, Lenoir. Lack of charm. The difference between a common thug and a skilled thief."

"I'm not here to take lessons from you. Cough up, or your new acquaintances will hear enough about your past deeds to make their blood curdle."

She shook her head. This didn't make sense. Nicolas was Guy's friend, a charming and intelligent man, and the coarseness of his speech was most unlike him. Still, what could he possibly have done that was so atrocious?

"You'd risk exposing yourself?"

"I don't care about these people," Lenoir sniffed. "I can always find another mark."

"And what if I simply smash your face in?" Nicolas's voice had dropped an octave, growing cold and menacing—almost the voice of a different person. A shiver ran up her spine. "That would solve the problem nicely. Without any teeth left, you'd have a hard time telling your tales of horror."

"You wouldn't." Lenoir was defiant, but his delivery trembled with an edge of fear. "The Boneman. He knows who you are, and he'll take an eye for an eye. I'm still under his protection."

"Protection? You're his fucking *dog*, damn you," Nicolas spat with contempt, then paused. "Very well. I'll give you what I have. Twenty francs."

"Liar. You must have more than that. What would be your purpose of even attending a fancy house party, if not to play at the card table every night and fleece these sheep?"

"I'm not here to work."

"I don't care. Double the sum or I'll talk."

Lenoir's words rang like a foghorn amid her confusion. The conversation was about to end. If one of them saw her... Her heart racing, she retreated as quickly as she could, padding through the thick grass and holding her skirts to keep them from rustling, back to the porch and the laughing children, back to the busy street and the haberdashery.

After she found Lisette, they made their way back to the chateau, chatting about needlework. But she couldn't push away the memory of what she'd overheard. God above, she was going to have to tell someone.

Guy. Of course. No matter if the mere idea of speaking to him again twisted her stomach. Nicolas was in danger, and Guy was the only one who could help him.

Chapter Eight

GUY SWEPT HIS neck with a kerchief before swatting it at a large fly that had landed on his horse's croup. The hour was nearing noon and he'd been riding since early that morning. His mount certainly didn't deserve such punishing exercise given the heat, however much Guy himself needed it, and the beast was well lathered. So when the stable boy had rushed into courtyard upon their return, Guy had insisted on unsaddling the horse himself and cooling him down with a walk. It was the least he could do.

And a fine beast he was, too, Guy reflected as he led him back to the courtyard to groom him. After tying the lead to a ring, he ran his palm over the powerful shoulder and neck, then picked up a brush and passed it over glossy withers. Perhaps he ought to ask François for advice on how to acquire such a horse for himself, which breeders were trustworthy and where he could fetch the best price. But he flicked the thought away almost immediately. Buying a horse, especially a good one, meant finding the right stable to accommodate it. It meant stability. Dependability. Commitment.

Sooner or later, you're going to have to settle down, his father had told him once. More than once, in fact, the exact wording varied little. *Commit yourself to your work, find a woman to marry, establish your own household. Occupy your time with expanding your mind and making the family business prosper, instead of riding at breakneck speed through the countryside and chasing girls.*

Hard blue eyes staring down at him, back as straight as a rod, hands forever manipulating papers and quills. Books and accounts, honor and duty. Those were the only things that had mattered to Joseph de Cazal. Had he clung to them until the very end, with his wife and his son fled to another country, and him climbing up wooden steps of the scaffold to meet his fate, with nothing to accompany him to his final moments beyond the screams of a bloodthirsty crowd? Such a twisted notion of justice.

He firmly worked the brush over the horse's croup. What good had that stability and dependability been in the end, when the world around him burned?

Guy paused, squeezing his eyes shut against the agonizing tightness around his heart. Rage and bitterness and regret had put down deep, thorny roots, enough to make him wonder if he'd ever dislodge them. The horse pawed at the ground, and Guy started up again, on the barrel this time, his taut nerves relaxing into the soothing, repetitive rhythm of the motion.

Since his return to France, he'd clutched at the conviction that peace was only a temporary reprieve, that blood would once again flow, red and fresh between the cobblestones of Paris. When, or how, or why, the details didn't matter. In whatever manner, death would descend upon them again, but this time he would make different choices. He would face danger, because this time, he would no longer have anything to lose.

Except Antonia had returned to his life. For months, his evenings had been replete with fine wines and witty conversation, his nights lost in musky beds and comely smiles, and his days, for the few hours when he was awake, spent riding and fighting and dallying. And yet, it was she—*she*—who allowed him to enjoy the heat of the sun, the coolness of fresh sheets, the potent tang of alcohol.

Delighted, agitated, inebriated, infuriated. Too much, all at once, and yet he couldn't stop. Thinking about her, wanting her. He was sick with it, and every time he saw her, he was reminded that the cure was right there, forever just beyond his reach.

He snorted, wiping his sweaty brow with his forearm, then looking down at his sodden, stained shirt. What a pathetic, miserable fool he was. Drowning in unspent lust and self-pity, his heart lurching and his groin clenching every time she walked into a room, bringing her loveliness and her smiles and her subtle, flowery scent with her.

Devil take it, he'd even started sympathizing with De Brienne, of all people, a sure sign of his declining mental state. He and Nicolas had mocked the poor bastard with unabashed relish when they'd see him trail behind Victoire at parties and catch him looking at her with eyes that reminded one of a wounded pup when she flirted with another man. And Guy took merciless pleasure in being the very one Victoire flirted with. De Brienne was the sort of man who believed his vast wealth gave him the right to treat those with lesser funds as lesser people; he'd been particularly vocal in denouncing Nicolas's presence at certain events, given his modest origins, and had enjoined others to give him the cut. Perfectly legitimate grounds for retaliation.

Guy ran the bristly brush over the horse's flanks. If not for Antonia's presence, it was possible—probable, if he were being honest—that he would've bedded Victoire during the house party and reveled in meeting De Brienne the next day at luncheon, knowing the man might suspect he had been cuckolded but would never be certain. Now he wouldn't wish this misery on his worst enemy.

At last, he dropped the brush and stepped back to appraise his work. The horse's coat was clean and lustrous now, but Guy didn't feel any better. Maybe a nice cold bath would help him clear his head and cool his blood.

But just as he was about to grab the riding coat he'd left hanging on the door of a stall, he spotted Antonia crossing the courtyard. Heading straight toward him.

Blast. Why was she seeking him out? His heart thumped painfully in his rib cage. If she had come to tell him that she was going back to Chartres this very minute, or that Rouget had suddenly grown some bollocks and declared himself and she was set to marry him within a fortnight, so help him God, he would get down on his knees in the dirt and beg her to reconsider.

No. She deserved better than that. She deserved that he wish her well, even as regret and fury ate him alive.

However, the expression on her face was not one of defiance or anger or coldness. The way she was frowning and glancing over her shoulder, her hands clasped together... She was worried. Apprehension rippled through his gut.

She slowed as she approached him and hesitated before speaking. "François told me I might find you here. I'm sorry to bother you..."

"You're not bothering me," he replied, and patted the horse's neck. "I just finished grooming him."

A small smile flickered across her lips and she reached out to place her palm on the soft, velvety muzzle. "You've always been so good with horses. *Papa* used to say he never saw anyone so at ease on a saddle, or more capable of handling an ill-tempered mount."

Because unlike people, horses weren't hard to understand, or to reason with. He shrugged. "Just a question of working with them and not against them."

"Funny. That's the same principle your father applied to his business, isn't it?"

"Perhaps, but that's the extent of the resemblance," he said dryly, hopefully cutting short any further reminiscences about his father. "What was it you wanted to speak to me about?"

"Oh. Well... this is a rather delicate matter."

Antonia let her hand drop and he resisted the urge to take it in his. "Whatever it is, you can..." *Trust me.* "... tell me. I'll do whatever is in my power to help."

"It's about Nicolas. And Monsieur Lenoir."

He paused and tightened his fists, then motioned to the stable boy to take the horse to its stall. "Come."

He led her behind the stables, next to an old well, hidden from view of the castles. He was careful to keep his distance from her; no need to remind himself what had happened last time he and Antonia had been together in a secluded area.

Protected by the shade of the eaves, Antonia took off her hat and fanned herself, her cheeks flushed. It was taking every gram of self-control Guy had not to rake his eyes over her face, her lips, her body, to fully drink in her proximity. Instead, he stared at the well.

"I was in the village," she started. "I overheard Lenoir and Nicolas. Lenoir mentioned… something Nicolas did in the past. Something awful, apparently."

Something awful. Lenoir could have been talking about any number of Nicolas's past misdeeds. He waited for her to go on.

"I know Nicolas is your friend, and he seems like a good man, intelligent and courteous, but… Do you know anything about this?"

No more lies. Not to her. And hell if he knew exactly what Lenoir was talking about. However, he wasn't about to reveal anything Nicolas had told him either.

"He's never kept anything from me, and never pretended to be someone he isn't," he simply said. "But his past belongs to him alone. Whatever he may have done is of no importance."

"It is to Lenoir," Antonia replied. "He's trying to blackmail Nicolas. He said that if Nicolas didn't hand over a significant sum of money, he'd tell everyone here what he'd done. And he's been taking advantage of Baptiste as well."

Of course. He'd sensed from the start that Lenoir was a shifty character. That he seemed out of place. It made perfect sense that Rouget was a mark.

"In fact, I should warn Claudine, she needs to tell her son to stay away from—"

"Wait."

If Nicolas hadn't already reduced the cur to a pile of broken bones, that meant Lenoir had some powerful allies, allies who revolved in the dark, treacherous world of Palais Royal brothels and gambling hells. Nicolas's world, though his friend sometimes longed to escape it. And after what he'd done for Guy…

"I'll take care of Lenoir," he stated.

Antonia reached out as if she meant to touch his arm but drew back at the last moment. His chest contracted and loosened into a breath. "He sounds like a ruthless man," she said. "He could harm you."

True. Lenoir certainly wasn't carrying around a loaded pistol, but a knife was easy to conceal in a sleeve. Good thing Nicolas had taught him how to disarm a man with a blade. But he couldn't admit as much to Antonia: this time, the concern in her eyes was for *him*. He would much rather face her cold indifference; at least that somewhat reined in his desire to kiss her. He returned to his thorough observation of the well.

"Lenoir has nothing on me. And if he's resorting to blackmail, that means he's in a position of weakness, not of power."

"Still…"

"Please. Don't trouble yourself. I'll watch him carefully before doing anything. If he doesn't suspect anyone is on to him, he'll act carelessly and set his own trap."

She sighed. "I hope you're right. I… I wouldn't want you in any danger."

A tense silence grew between them and he grasped for a change of subject.

"What were you doing in the village?"

Antonia fanned herself more quickly. "Lisette, my maid, wanted to buy supplies. Ribbons, in particular. She means to wear some tonight. Everyone is very excited for the Feast of Saint John, naturally."

"And will you be joining in the festivities?"

Might as well brace himself now, if he was to see her on Rouget's arm while he shadowed Lenoir.

"I'm not sure. I feel a bit of a headache coming on."

Relief swept through him, followed by remorse at the idea that she might be depriving herself of the celebration on purpose, in order to avoid him. He nodded shortly.

"Right. Better get back inside and avoid the sun, then. Do you wish me to accompany you back to the chateau?"

"No, but it's kind of you to offer," she replied. A peculiar wistfulness lingered in her tone. "Guy… be careful. I beg of you."

By God, she shouldn't be begging him for anything. He bit his lip and remained in closed silence until she finally left.

⋙✦⋘

FLAMES FROM THE bonfire twisted their way toward the darkened sky, seeming to dance in time with the merry tune coming from a nearby musical group. Revelers cavorted in the flickering light, darting in familiar patterns under the stars, while others chatted in small groups, men and women no doubt using the cover of the deepening night to secure an assignation.

On any other evening, Guy would have happily joined them. But not tonight. Tonight, he had only one quarry, and that was Lenoir.

His gaze darted through the crowd. If the bastard wished to embarrass Nicolas, he could certainly take advantage of the gathered celebrants and spread his message to as many ears as possible. So far, Lenoir had kept moving. Buying spiced wine from a merchant, talking to Rouget.

Biding his time, perhaps. Waiting for the right moment to strike. And now, with every step he was edging his way through the crowd toward the worst person possible.

Victoire.

Good God, no. If Lenoir managed to convince *her* of his story, he wouldn't have to blare it like a priest calling the banns on Sunday. Victoire possessed a vicious enough tongue for gossip that she would gladly spread the story for him, and a few days certainly sufficed for anyone, let alone a swindler like Lenoir, to understand that she took immense pleasure in being the center of attention.

He chanced a glance at Nicolas, who was standing a little apart, with Claudine hanging on his arm, laughing at something he had just said. Nicolas might well have been charming the older woman with some wild tale, but Guy knew better. The way Nicolas's gaze darted about the gathering every so often told that his old friend was every bit as much on the alert.

But Guy stood closer to Lenoir. He could head this off. Shouldering his way past a laughing couple, never once taking his eyes off Lenoir, he pushed toward Victoire. For an instant, his gaze crossed that of Lenoir, and Guy made no effort to hide his animosity.

Something in his expression must have shown even through the shadows, for Lenoir abruptly changed direction.

Guy followed, the crowd thinning as they made their way out of the village square, past the church, taking the road... bloody hell, Lenoir was taking the road back toward the chateau. With the servants all at the feast, barely anyone was left. Lenoir would have free rein to go through any room he wanted. He must have figured out this would be a quicker, more efficient way to get the funds he needed.

Had he found out where Nicolas's room was in order to ransack it? Stealing something from someone else's possessions would be much too risky. But if he was going in blind, or if he made a mistake, if he entered another room...

Antonia.

She was almost entirely alone in the chateau. Unprotected. Unaware of the danger fast approaching. Sleeping softly in her bed.

Pure, white-hot rage erupted inside him at the thought of a vicious scoundrel laying but a finger on her. No. Guy took a breath in a vain attempt to calm his senses, all of which were screaming for him to surge forth and go straight for the jugular. No. If he attacked him here, the craven could flee in the dark, disappear, strike later. If he waited until they reached the chateau, he could ensure that Lenoir would vacate the premises.

Guy waited to a slow count to ten before he set off again, placing distance between him and his prey. Best to let the man lower his guard, think himself free of pursuit. The longer Guy followed, the closer they got to the ornate, ironwork gates and the broad drive that led to the estate, the more his instincts urged him to act, but still he held back.

He held himself in check as far as the formal garden. The fountain splashed and played in a ray of moonlight. Romantic to a fault. Too bad he was here for something entirely less pleasant than a tryst.

"Lenoir!"

The other man froze. Pivoted. "What the hell are you doing here?"

"Funny, I was about to ask you the same question." He made a show of cracking his knuckles. "Planning on emptying some drawers and making off with your loot while everyone is down in the village?"

"What's it to you?" Lenoir's stance seemed relaxed, yet tension crackled in the air, like far-off lightning that signaled an impending storm.

"You threaten my friends, you threaten me."

"Is this about Lefevre?" Lenoir sneered. "Is he too much of a milksop to fight his own battles? My word, his bollocks have shriveled up, keeping company with gutless bourgeois like you."

Fury coursed through Guy's limbs, tensing his muscles, screaming to be released. "Nicolas could smash your nose into your fucking skull with a slap of his wrist."

"Really? Is that why he sends—" Lenoir looked Guy over from head to toe, his expression dripping in contempt—"a pretty-faced rich boy to do the job?" He squared his feet, bracing in readiness, his hands raised. "Come on then. If you want me to bloody the pavement with your face, I'll be glad to oblige, *monsieur*."

"Right." Guy tore off his coat and advanced on his adversary. "Let me show you how a gutless bourgeois gets the job done."

⇸⟫⟫⟫⟪⟪⟪⇷

ANTONIA TOSSED AND turned in her bed, stuffing her pillow under her head, trying to find a cool spot on the soft linen. Hot. It was too hot. No, that wasn't the problem. The sheets, her nightrail, all of it tangled in her legs, made her too aware of her own skin.

Sleep. Sleep. She threw her arm over her eyes. Maybe if she let her mind drift... To a pair of deep blue eyes, strong hands, a broad chest...

Bad idea. That was the opposite of calming.

Desperate for rest, she started to run the story of *Pamela* in her head, chapter by chapter, and was finally drifting in a no-land on the very edge of consciousness when shouts ripped her back to reality. Revelers returning from the festivities in the village already?

No. Those cries had been fueled by anger.

She sat up, threw the sheets back. A dull *thwack* that sounded suspiciously like flesh striking flesh had her bolting out of bed toward the window.

The scene that met her eyes made her blood run cold. She bit down on a fist to stop the scream that clawed its way up her throat.

Guy was down in the yard, exchanging blows with Lenoir. And not simple blows with their fists. Guy's foot whipped through the air and smashed into Lenoir's ribs. The impact ought to have sent the other man reeling. Somehow he absorbed it and countered with a vicious swing that struck Guy in the belly.

His breath expelled in a rush, carrying curses audible even from the second story. He staggered, and Antonia's stomach plummeted. In the next instant, his feet planted, and heel whipped out, impossibly high, aimed directly for Lenoir's head.

With an evil leer, Lenoir dodged, countered. Then the fight seemed to pause, and the men circled, assessing, each coiled in anticipation of the next move. Blood oozed from a cut over Guy's eyebrow to trickle down the side of his cheek. He spat on the ground, squared his muscular shoulders, ready for the next assault.

This was brutal. It was barbaric. It should offend every last one of her civilized sensibilities. Instead, it sent darts of heat through her breasts and deeper into her very core. That spot Guy had teased with his fingers seemed to swell and throb and made her wish for those same fingers again—*there*—those same fingers that even now were clenched into weapons to rain destruction on Lenoir's face.

She shook her head. Enough.

This had to stop. Now. Before someone—*before Guy*—was killed.

She whirled away from the window, her nightrail floating about her bare legs. No time for propriety. She rushed down the stairs and out the door to the terrace just in time to catch the shimmer of something metallic slipping into Lenoir's hand.

The pale light from the moon glinted off a knife blade.

"Guy!"

She regretted the warning as soon as it left her mouth. Face contorted into a feral snarl, Guy glanced in her direction. At the same moment the knife curved upward in an arc aimed for his heart.

Just before the blade sank into his chest, Guy pivoted left, his hand clamping down on Lenoir's forearm, twisting until he held Lenoir pinioned. With a cry, Lenoir let the knife drop. With a sweep of his foot, Guy sent Lenoir hurtling to the dirt, his body following, to land with his full weight on top of the downed man.

For a moment, only their harsh breathing broke the night's silence, then Guy seized him by the collar and punched him square in the face.

"Had enough, you whoreson?" he growled.

"I yield," Lenoir whimpered. "I yield."

Guy didn't relent. He looked like he might not let go until the man was cold on the pavement.

"Guy," Antonia called helplessly. "Please, come back."

Finally, his fingers slowly uncurled. He picked up the blade that lay on the ground beside Lenoir and stood up, blood still flowing from his brow onto his white shirt.

"You have an hour to gather your things and leave," he rasped. "I'll summon whichever domestic was asked to stand guard in the chateau and have them assist you. If you're still here past that time, I will kill you. With your own knife."

Lenoir nodded, scrambling to his feet and away from him, his lip split into an oozing mess. Guy turned away and started toward the steps of the terrace, his pace almost sluggish, as if the roaring energy that had sustained him during the fight was now seeping out of him. She rushed down to meet him.

"Are you all right? *Seigneur*, your wound… The blood…"

Guy shook his head. "It's fine. I'm fine."

But when he set his foot on the first step, his knees buckled.

"Here, lean against me," she said, and lifted his arm to put it around her shoulder. "I'll help you to your room. You'll feel better once I've cleaned up your brow."

Chapter Nine

THE STRIP OF linen laying in the basin on the nightstand stained the water red. Antonia reached out to push the dark, damp strands of hair from Guy's brow. At long last, the wound had stopped bleeding, and cleaning it had revealed it to be shallow. She let herself breathe more easily. Here, in the intimate dimness of his room, nothing could happen to him.

"I gather you will be bombarded with questions tomorrow, but seeing as Claudine and Baptiste must be told what Lenoir was up to, it's hardly a matter for discretion."

Guy nodded shortly, the candlelight drawing long shadows on his chiseled features. He was sitting on his bed, his pillow propped against the headboard, his expression solemn.

"Are you all right now?" she asked.

"You shouldn't worry so, Antonia," he muttered. "I'm not worth the trouble."

"What are you talking about? When I saw him with that knife, I thought..." Unspilled tears seared her eyes. "You could have been *killed*."

He didn't contradict her. Instead, he simply took her hand and threaded his fingers with hers.

"Anyone who's seen you and Nicolas together can see what a dear friend he is to you," she went on, dread roiling within her, "but to *die* for him?"

"I owe him my life."

The statement lingered in the air between them. Though her throat constricted again at the thought of Guy facing mortal danger, she wasn't surprised. If he'd learned to fight in this brutal manner, he must have had a good reason to do so.

He looked down at their entwined hands. "When I returned to France, I headed straight to Paris, in order to try and reclaim my father's deeds. The Revolutionary Tribunal had taken everything after we fled for Switzerland—his properties, his fortune. Everything."

His tone was dull, almost factual, but not enough to conceal the emotion that simmered underneath. "I was alone, of course. Alone and lost. I would've been the perfect mark for someone like Lenoir, had I any real money to spend. But as it was, I didn't need anyone to show me the way to gambling hells and... other places of ill repute."

He abruptly dropped her hand and crossed his arms over his chest. Antonia looked away, shifting awkwardly, not knowing what to do with her arms and legs. She didn't want to think of Guy in that sort of establishment. His expression, however, was not one of fond remembrance—quite the opposite, in fact.

"One night, I was at the same card table as Nicolas, in one of the seedier hells of Palais Royal. I thought one of the other players had cheated, challenged him to a fight, though I was in no condition to land a single punch on anyone. I was so deep in my cups I didn't realize I was signing my own death warrant." He shook his head. "We ended up in the street, the man had a knife... Nicolas grabbed his arm just as the blade was about to sink into my gut. If he hadn't followed us outside, I'd have ended up a corpse on the pavement."

Antonia could only gape at him. How far had he fallen to end up in such a dreadful state? And why? They were edging toward that forbidden, inscrutable period of his life, those ten years that were cloaked in complete darkness. She pressed her lips against the urge to ask one of the multitude of questions that whirled in her mind, waiting for him to go on.

The ghost of a smile passed over his lips. "To this day, I don't know why Nicolas followed me. There was nothing to distinguish me from any of the other wretches who were gambling their souls away that night. After he chased off the other man, we sat down together, started to talk… Talked until dawn, in fact. He offered to teach me how to fight. If I was going to survive in Palais Royal, he told me, I ought to know how to defend myself."

Thinking back on the way he had pummeled Lenoir, she could only agree with him, though he would no doubt be surprised to learn it had elicited other feelings in her than admiration, ones that didn't bear mentioning. Especially now, with the two of them sitting so close, she in her delicate nightrail, he in a fresh shirt he had only slipped on, she suspected, to make her feel less uncomfortable.

"Well, he's a very good teacher indeed," she said, her voice catching in her throat.

"Under his supervision, I trained during the day, and in the evenings, we watched out for each other, worked in tandem," Guy continued. "We quickly developed a skill to enter more pleasant venues than those of Palais Royal. Nicolas, because of his wit and charm, and I, because of my name, and the funds that were starting to trickle back in."

Not to mention his striking looks. Yes, no doubt that must have helped greatly in gaining entry in the Parisian *beau monde*. She shivered, once again reminded of how very little she was wearing.

"Indeed, Claudine informed me that the two of you had a reputation for burning the candle at both ends."

"Yes. And look where it got me." He lowered his gaze and fell silent for a moment. "You were right when you called me a *débauché*."

Yes, she had meant the words when she'd spoken them. And she'd clung to her anger like a shield, the only thing keeping her afloat in a sea of yearning and confusion. But looking at him now, battered and exhausted, his blue eyes filled with torment, her anger crumbled, leaving only a sorrowful tenderness.

"No. A *débauché* doesn't care about anyone, or anything. You care."

Too much so, in fact. She placed her hand on his cheek, and he kept it there, closing his eyes and leaning into her palm as if he meant to rest against it. She leaned over and pressed her lips tenderly to his.

"Get some sleep," she murmured.

"Only if you stay with me."

She withdrew her hand and placed it on her lap. "What? I can't. It's.... not proper."

Even to her ears, the excuse sounded ridiculous. None of this was proper. In fact, she had done more improper things since arriving here than she'd done in her entire life. The truth was, she wanted to stay. Tonight, tomorrow, and all the days after that. She couldn't bear the idea of them being parted again. And that was the whole problem.

"Please, Antonia. I won't be able to sleep if I don't know you're safe."

He was drifting off. Her shaky resolve swayed and toppled. She couldn't just leave him now.

Climbing fully onto the bed, she took the other pillow and lay down next to him, staring at the flickering candlelight before sinking into a deep slumber.

⟫⟫≪≪

WHEN ANTONIA OPENED her eyes, the soft gray light of early dawn filled the room. The chateau was plunged in the still, soothing silence of the early hours, and she was ensconced in delicious warmth.

Guy. He'd rolled to his side during the few hours they'd been asleep, and she was nestled against him, her back to his front, as if a place had been carved out in his body just for her. His arm draped over her waist and his hand lay curled next to hers on the cover, slightly bruised at the knuckles, now relaxed in sleep.

It was the sweetest, most perfect sensation she'd ever known. She closed her eyes again, listening to his deep, steady breaths, feeling his chest rise and fall against her back.

Alive. Both of them, alive and together and safe, after enduring so many hardships. Nothing short of a miracle.

For a few minutes, she let herself bask in it, drinking it in, letting it wash away brittle shards of anguish and insecurity. She was in Guy's arms, and the fires and music and fighting had vanished, ceding their place to a serene dawn. The world had stopped moving. There were only the two of them, here and now.

Behind her, Guy shifted. His arm tightened around her waist, bringing her closer still, and a dense, rigid length pressed against her backside.

Oh. The last traces of sleep immediately left her. Could a man be so aroused in a state of slumber? Or had Guy woken up? She should try to untangle herself. Go back to her room before anyone saw her, before she did something she would later regret. Before this heady, thick pulse of want grew too strong to stop, too intoxicating to escape…

Too late. The ache in her core was already swelling, spurred by the hard press of his erection against her curves, and the unshakable image of it filling the emptiness inside. Her heart beating wildly, she arched back, tentatively at first, then more firmly, awaiting his reaction.

His breathing changed. Rougher, shallower. Yes, he was definitely awake now. His hips rolled forward and she gave a soft whimper.

"Antonia," he murmured next to her ear, then kissed the nape of her neck. Light as a feather, but enough to send a long, slow shiver through her body. "You're so soft…" Another kiss. "So warm…" Another. "*Hmmm… Heaven.*"

A whole trail of kisses descended on her shoulders, her back. *Stop him. Stop him now.* But she couldn't. It was like trying to stop the roiling currents of a stream come springtime. The heady, irrepressible swell was gathering in her breasts, between her thighs, making her squirm and writhe, urging words of wanton abandon up her throat, the very same that had delivered her when last she'd felt this agony.

"Please, Guy," she whispered. "Put your hands on me. Like the other night."

He paused, and she felt him grin against her skin. "My sweet, virtuous love. How quickly you've learned to ask for what you want."

His hand snaked up to cup her breast, and heat rushed to her nipples, gathering in a tight bundle. The muslin was so thin she might as well have been wearing nothing at all, but still he dipped past the neckline, squeezing, pulling, pinching the sensitive tip until her lips parted in a mewling sigh.

"Does this please you?" he teased her.

"Yes… *oh*… that's lovely."

His touch left her breast, only to slide under the rumpled hem of her nightrail and up her thighs.

"And this?"

Antonia gasped as his fingers brushed against her folds and slid along the dewy crease, finding the exact rhythm, the precise spot that set her entire body aflame. He dipped the tip of his forefinger into her—*yes*, oh goodness, she had already experienced *this* exquisite pleasure—but then retrieved it, taunting her with more deft caresses.

"Don't stop," she begged. "I need… I need…"

"I know exactly what you need, love. I can feel it right there."

Oh, it was maddening. Why wasn't he allowing her to reach her peak? She tilted the angle of her hips, to no avail, only succeeding in increasing the friction with his hardened length. *This.* This was what she craved. This would finally relieve the frenzied, burning ache he was stoking with each swipe of his fingers.

Yet how could she make such a demand?

"Guy." She squeezed her eyes shut. "It hurts. Inside."

He immediately stilled his hand. "I'm hurting you?"

"No, no, I meant to say..." No other way around it. It made it a bit easier, not having to look at him while she spoke. "It hurts because I want you. All of you. I want you so much, it feels like I might die from it."

He emitted a sound halfway between a moan and a growl. His hand left her. "Turn around."

She rolled to her back, finally facing him. The look on his face knocked the breath out of her. Ravenous. Determined. And his blue eyes almost black with a storm of arousal.

His full lips met hers in a searing kiss, biting and devouring, holding nothing back, and she twined her arms around his neck. Small barbs of doubt cut through her feverish desire. Should she part her legs now? Did he have enough room to undo his breeches? Would there be pain from the start? She tensed.

Guy broke away. "Are you well?"

She hesitated. The most common advice she'd heard on the topic was simply to bear the first attempts in silence, as well as one could. Maybe Guy would think she was silly for voicing her concerns. Yet he'd stilled his hand when he thought he was hurting her. And now he was stroking her cheek in a soothing motion, silently encouraging her to answer.

"I was told to expect... discomfort."

"Yes, at first. But not for long. And much less if a lover has been attentive beforehand."

"Oh. So I shouldn't trouble myself, as you have been most attentive."

The corners of his mouth lifted into a playful smile that made her heart flutter. "Not nearly enough." He bent down to kiss her again. "Will you let me pleasure you with my mouth?"

Vivid memories of the way his tongue had swirled over the

tip of her breasts flashed through her mind and she nodded eagerly. He trailed his mouth down the slope of her neck and nudged her loose neckline aside to suck at the pebbled buds, but to her surprise, he didn't linger. Instead, he kept going lower... And lower... Lifting her hem over her thighs, her waist...

Suddenly, his intent became clear, and the shock of realization made her close her legs. Having Guy see her so closely, so intimately... Yes, the pulsing want between her legs yearned for his mouth, but it was fighting a hard battle with apprehension.

A stinging blush rose to her face. "I'm not certain you should do that."

He set his head on her stomach, idly tracing his finger up and down her thigh. "Really? Whyever not?"

To her relief, he didn't sound angry, or impatient. Simply curious. Still, she threw her arm over her face, too embarrassed to look at him.

"Antonia," he said. "Let me put you at ease. Tell me what it is you fear."

"That you will find me..." *Repulsive.* "... lacking."

His burst of laughter sent a ripple through her belly. "I guarantee you, love, that is impossible. If you knew how arousing it is for me to uncover the beautiful pearl you keep tucked away, just there... To kiss it, to please it with my tongue... To hear all the lovely sounds you will make when I do..."

As he talked, her legs relaxed and fell apart of their own accord. How was she to resist this man, the smooth warmth of his voice, and now the firm heat of his mouth? He parted her and teased her gently at first, swirling around the spot that was most sensitive before increasing the pressure of his tongue. Nervous tickles soon gave way to something else, something dark and primitive and exhilarating.

He broke away and nipped at her thigh. "Do you still want me to stop?"

"No. No, it's..." She broke off in a small cry. "It's so good."

He put his mouth on her again, licking her with undisguised

relish, lapping at her, suckling the swollen, sensitive nub from which all of her pleasure unfurled. Heavens above, nothing this sinful should be this pleasurable, should make her feel like she was at once leaving her own skin and being tethered by a single point in her body. She moaned. She begged. She didn't care, so long as this never stopped.

"Guy... Please, keep going, please... Oh... *oh...*"

He thrust a finger into her. Then a second, up to the knuckle. Her muscles shuddered with a sudden rush of sheer, unfettered bliss, careening through her limbs, making her jerk against him and tearing a hoarse cry from her chest.

For a few seconds, she lay limp on the cover, struggling to catch her breath. Struggling to think beyond the ecstasy she had just experienced. Finally, she managed to prop herself up on her elbows.

Guy stood beside the bed and pulled off his shirt. Her eyes roamed over his lean, sculpted chest, every muscle defined to perfection, and caught the smattering of dark hairs that led inside his breeches.

A moment later, he shucked them off, and she took in the sight of his engorged manhood. Her nervousness returned—what if it was simply too large to fit? Yet she didn't look away. An irrepressible, compelling force had taken control of her. The ache, the emptiness, the need for him was so acute it numbed all other considerations.

"Take off your nightrail. Let me see all of you."

His voice was deeper, commanding. She sat up on the bed, trembling, and divested herself of the flimsy gown. His stare turned ravenous.

"My God, you are beautiful."

He returned next to her on the bed. Barely controlled tension was coming off his toned body, enveloping her, rekindling her desire. He placed a hand on her stomach.

"If you have concerns regarding the natural consequences this may have, rest assured I will be cautious to avoid them. However, it isn't entirely failsafe, so if you've changed your mind…"

"No."

She couldn't bear it if they stopped now.

"Then I will make you mine, Antonia. Mine entirely."

I'm already yours.

He kissed her, mingling his tongue with hers, positioning himself at her entrance. Searing pain shot through her as he pushed inside of her, centimeter by centimeter, breaking the kiss to groan in the crook of her neck. She willed herself to stay calm, as fretting and wincing would certainly make things worse, but she couldn't help a whimper when he finally plunged all the way in.

He lifted his head to gaze into her eyes. Could he see the swirling wave of emotion that was rising in her in spite of the pain?

For she loved Guy. It wasn't just her body driving her to give herself to him. It was her mind, her memories of the past and her hopes for the future, her soul. She loved him so much, she would take the pain, the hurt, all of it, a thousand times over, because she couldn't fathom taking them for any other man.

He pressed his forehead against hers and started to move again, slowly at first. "Is this all right?"

She nodded, locked her eyes with his and dug her fingers into his back. "Keep going."

His pace accelerated, filling her with his taut, masculine hardness, over and over again, until she could sense the breathtaking pleasure it would bring her once the sharp burn subsided.

"By God, this is too good," he panted, then bent over to kiss her. "Too good."

He thrust more forcefully, his breath harsh and rapid between his open lips. A loud groan tore from his throat as he brusquely pulled out of her. Hot wetness spilled onto her thighs, and Guy slumped into her arms.

"*Seigneur,*" he rasped. "That was… exquisite. Not long enough by half. But exquisite."

She played with the soft hair curling at the nape of his neck. "Shall we try again, then?"

He gave a little laugh. "You are insatiable. But I'm going to need a few minutes to gather my strength. And you are far too sore for now. We had best wait until…"

Until when? Suddenly, the light of the sun appeared more glaring. She could hear footsteps and the hushed noises of servants starting their day, on the other side of the door. There was no escaping the day.

"Tonight," he concluded. "Tonight, love, I will properly show you the extent of my capacities."

He rolled off of her and grazed his thumb over her swollen lips. "In the meantime, let me clean you up and help you dress. With a bit of luck, you'll able to slip back into your room without anyone being the wiser."

He was right, of course. But even though it was only for a few hours, leaving him now left her feeling wistful and forlorn.

What would happen, then, when in two days the party would end and she would have to leave him for far longer?

She pushed the thought back mercilessly. Yet she knew it only lay dormant, biding its time to strike again.

Chapter Ten

"A STORM IS gathering, is it not?"

Guy followed Rouget's gaze beyond the balustrade of the terrace to the horizon. The light gray clouds veiling the sky grew darker above the trees, and the air was thick with humidity. Claudine patted her bosom with a kerchief and glanced up sharply from her glass of tonique at her son, who seemed to shrink under her gaze.

"Don't try to change the subject. How could you be so naive as to let yourself be fooled in this manner? Haven't I taught you better?"

Rouget gave a pleading look to Guy and Nicolas, who were standing with him next to the table. Nicolas patted his shoulder and turned to Claudine.

"In his defense, *madame*, it seems to me that Monsieur Lenoir is rather skilled at deception. These swindlers hone their technique over many years, and people with far more experience and acumen than Monsieur Rouget have been duped in a similar manner."

"Besides, it was just a bit of fun, a few francs here and there," Rouget added. "It's not as if I ruined the family with a colossal gambling debt."

Her dark eyes flashed, and for the first time, Guy sensed the full force of a woman who had to raise four unruly boys to be respectable gentlemen. "And I should *thank* you for that?"

"No, that's not what I—"

"If anyone here should be thanked, it's Monsieur de Cazal, who courageously stopped that villain before he could rob us blind!"

Guy ignored Nicolas's pointed stare and bowed his head. "I was only doing my duty, *madame*."

"But how fortunate that you saw Lenoir slipping away, and that you had the mind to follow him." She took a gulp of tonique and her eyes watered. "Having him rifle through our drawers would have been bad enough, but to think what could have happened if he'd harmed our precious Antonia, who was sleeping like a babe in her room…"

Indeed. And whenever he did think of it, the bloodlust returned intact. But Lenoir couldn't harm Antonia now. No one would ever harm her, or even touch her. No one but him. *Mine entirely.* The thought sent a thrill of elation through him.

"It was nothing, I assure you."

Claudine sighed. "He did leave a nasty bruise on your brow. Though I must say, *monsieur*, it doesn't take anything away from your dashing looks, on the contrary."

"*Maman!*" Rouget gasped. "I beg of you—"

"Hush," she interrupted him. "Another word and I'll cuff your ear. Now where *is* Antonia, I wonder? I thought she would be up before us, seeing as she went to bed early. It's past eleven."

Nicolas raised an eyebrow. "Indeed. But elegant young ladies have a delicate constitution and tire easily. If by chance she engaged in any strenuous exercise—"

"I'm sure she'll come down soon," Guy cut in before Nicolas could continue taunting him. "In the meantime, I have a book I wanted Monsieur Lefevre's opinion on. Excuse us while we retire to the library."

They took their leave of the Rougets and went inside. Guy elbowed Nicolas in the ribs and he gave a pained laugh.

"Go easy. I don't want to end up like Lenoir. I'm only sorry I couldn't see that bastard's face when you were done with him."

Was he mistaken, or was that pride on Nicolas's face? He shrugged his shoulders. "Hopefully he spit out a few teeth before he left."

They strolled along the gallery to the library, enjoying the placid silence. Most guests were still in bed, recuperating from the previous evening's excesses.

"Tell me now," Nicolas finally said, "how did you find out?"

"Antonia overheard you and Lenoir. She came to see me. She was concerned for you."

"I should thank her. And you as well, for getting rid of that rat on my behalf, though it seems you've already been handsomely rewarded for your efforts. So, how was it?"

They shared a glance and Guy grinned. "Words would fall short to describe it."

And he had no desire to try, either. On occasion he and Nicolas had shared detailed accounts of their livelier trysts, but he wanted to keep the ecstasy of that pale gray dawn in Antonia's arms all to himself.

"I suppose you're not going to claim your prize."

Guy frowned. "What prize?"

"The wager."

He startled. He had completely forgotten about it. "I've already won the best prize there is. At this point I'd rather go for another round with Lenoir than discuss the terms of that damn wager with Victoire."

"Can't say that I blame you. They say no man ever rejected Madame Le Plessis Tailland, but perhaps that's because no man who did ever lived to tell the story."

They arrived in front of the library before Guy could reply, and when he looked inside the room, all thoughts flew from his mind.

Antonia was standing next to the shelf, dressed in one of her pastel muslin frocks, her head bent over an open book. It was a pose he'd seen her take countless times, and for an instant he felt he had stepped into the past. But the present came rushing back when she raised her head. Eyes gleaming, cheeks like rose petals, plump lips curving into a smile. And this morning, all of her loveliness seemed to be for him and him alone. A warm glow bloomed from his chest to the rest of his body.

"Antonia," he said, his voice catching slightly. "Did you… rest well?"

"I did. And you?"

He nodded. The urge to rush over to her and kiss her was so overwhelming he had to keep his fists tightly clasped behind his back. Nicolas bowed in greeting.

"Good morning, Mademoiselle Saint Yves."

She blinked as if dazed and turned toward him with a graceful tilt of her head. "To you as well, Monsieur Lefevre."

Nicolas opened his mouth to reply, but Antonia's eyes had flitted back toward Guy, and he held them there with his own gaze, drinking in the sight of her.

"Forgive me," Nicolas said after a few moments, his tone wavering with contained laughter. "I must see to… something."

As soon as he had stepped out, Guy strode toward Antonia and gathered her in his arms, pressing his mouth to hers in a fevered kiss. If he had previously held the notion that bedding Antonia would assuage his need for her, it had evaporated. On the contrary, it had only made it worse.

"Guy," she breathed against his lips. "You mustn't. We're right in front of the window."

Yet she didn't pull away from his embrace. He touched his forehead to hers.

"How are you feeling? Are you sore?"

"A little," she admitted. "But I like being reminded of what we did, and… the way you felt inside of me."

Good Lord, he was this close to telling her to go back up to her room so he could join her there and continue right where they'd left off.

"You know, this morning, I thought how pleasant it would be to take you riding," he said, brushing her cheekbone with his thumb. "Then I remembered now may not be the best time."

Antonia's smile grew. "Oh, I would so enjoy it. Perhaps if we keep a slow pace... Or you could give me a tour of the stables. Show me how you tend that beautiful horse of yours."

"It's François's horse, but I'd be glad to demonstrate." He frowned slightly. "Are you sure you're interested?"

"Of course. No one ever bothered to explain any of these things to me. When I was younger, I was too scared to mount our horse or even drive him, so Papa and Jerome just assumed I was hopeless."

"Well, in that case..."

The sound of steps and voices coming down the gallery cut him off. Antonia rushed to put some distance between them.

"... and I can only hope your brothers will learn a lesson from all of this." Claudine and Baptiste appeared in the frame of the door. "Perhaps if you write to Pierrot—oh, my dear! There you are!"

Guy could only watch as Claudine swept Antonia up and made her listen to the tale of the fight she had in fact witnessed first-hand. She covered her knowledge well by making a great show of surprise at the most dramatic parts.

"I told Monsieur de Cazal that his bruise made him look quite debonair. Don't you agree?"

Antonia blushed to the root of her hair. "I—well, I suppose so."

Claudine laughed. "Dear me, I'm embarrassing you with my silly chatter. Come, let's go outside and play a *jeu de mail* before the rain comes."

Guy reluctantly followed behind Claudine and Antonia, doing his best to respond to Baptiste's extensive review of the different food stalls that had been set up in the village the previous evening and keeping his gaze fixed on the nape of Antonia's neck and the fine hair that curled there. By the time they had returned to the terrace, Marie-Louise and François were up as well, and they immediately assailed Guy with questions over last night's events. News apparently traveled fast in a chateau.

And so it went on, as more guests rose and joined the group that had gathered on the lawn, either to play *jeu de mail* or to watch the game. When Nicolas arrived, he took over telling the story, and Guy was free to simply watch Antonia's attempts at whacking the wooden ball with her mallet to hit a wicket.

Observing her, it occurred to him that what he had considered as inelegance and callowness when he was twenty was now precisely what charmed him. The easy, unaffected manner with which Antonia played, her burst of laughter and reddened cheeks, the way she kept pushing back the russet ringlets that escaped from her chignon, all of it elicited sensations he hadn't felt in a very long time.

Sensations that reminded him of happier times. Of home.

He closed his eyes for a moment, struggling against the wave of emotion that welled up within him. Something wet landed on his cheek.

"Oh drat, it's starting to rain," Claudine exclaimed.

Two other drops landed in his hair and on his hand. Seconds later, the guests were retreating in haste to avoid the imminent downpour. When they arrived in the parlor, they found Victoire half-lying on a lounge chair, draped in a silky sea-green dress that emphasized her unusual pallor, and De Brienne sitting next to her, patting her hand rather awkwardly.

"*Seigneur*, what racket you made outside," she snapped. "Not only did it wake me up, but now I have an ungodly headache."

"My valet always recommends an infusion of lavender and chamomile for such an affliction," De Brienne said. "Surely if we ask in the kitchens—"

Victoire gave a little sniff. "Why bother with an infusion when laudanum is so much more effective? Honestly, sometimes words come out of your mouth that make me wonder if you've taken leave of your senses."

"No, he's right," Guy said.

De Brienne and Victoire both glared at him.

"Lavender does soothe the pain. And one develops a tolerance to laudanum. If it's used too often for simple headaches, one must progressively increase the dose."

De Brienne couldn't have looked more surprised if Guy had grown a second head. He shifted uncomfortably. Blast, he should have shut his mouth. But he couldn't simply stand there and let Victoire walk all over that poor sod when he had the right of it.

Thunder rolled in the distance. Marie-Louise went to the window and despondently watched the sheets of rain coming down on the gardens. She turned away from the window and sighed.

"It'll last a while by the looks of it. But I suppose it was to be expected, after so many days of heat. Better today than yesterday, though."

Lightning flashed, followed by a loud clap a few seconds later, and a few guests startled in their seats.

"The storm is getting closer, it seems," Claudine remarked. "Why not play a game to keep ourselves entertained while it passes?"

Victoire raised her eyes to the heavens. "Please, let it not be charades. I'd die from sheer tedium."

Claudine's expression didn't falter. "Actually, I was about to suggest a few rounds of *cligne-musette*."

The room erupted in pleased murmurs and low laughs. Guy's mouth quirked into a smile. Nothing like *cligne-musette* to liven things up indeed. His gaze slipped toward Antonia. She was seated next to Rouget, and both of them listened politely, obviously unaware of what a child's game might hold in store when it was played by adults.

"The rules are simple," Claudine continued. "We'll draw straws to determine who starts as *le chat*. This person will then stand in a corner and count to a hundred, while the rest of us hide. The first person *le chat* finds will then join the hunt, and so on and so forth until everyone is found."

"What a delightful proposition," Nicolas said with a smile. "Pray tell, *madame*, is anything off limits? I mean, in terms of where we're allowed to hide."

Claudine's eyes sparkled with mirth. "Let us stay on the ground floor. No hiding in the bedrooms. And no locking doors, that wouldn't be fair," she added, wagging her finger at him.

Nicolas nonchalantly picked a bit of fluff off his sleeve. "Of course. The entire point is to get caught, is it not? That's what makes the game worth playing."

Claudine pressed her lips together, as if she was holding back a fit of giggles.

"Well, that sounds like fun," Rouget said, still oblivious to what was unfolding right in front of him. "Doesn't it, Mademoiselle Saint Yves?"

Antonia glanced at Guy and he held her gaze for a moment, making no effort to hide his desire for her. No, she should see it. Feel it. Know that he had gone without kissing her for entirely too long a time and counted on rectifying the situation as soon as possible. A rosy blush appeared on her cheeks and she turned back to Rouget.

"Yes, quite," she replied, a little breathless.

By God, he wanted to make her more breathless than that, hear her plead and sigh and mewl with pleasure like she had that morning when he'd brought her to her climax with his mouth. He'd never be able to wait until the evening. As soon as the game began, he'd go on a hunt of his own.

At Claudine's request, a footman bought them a bundle of straws. François cut one short before holding them in his fist for the guests to draw.

"You're it, Victoire!" Marie-Louise cried with delight as everyone held up their straw. "You drew the short straw!"

"Ridiculous," Victoire huffed. "I have half a mind to leave you all to your inane attempts at entertainment."

"But then who would be *le chat*?" Nicolas drawled. "You seem particularly well-suited in the role of pussy cat, *madame*."

De Brienne took her hand in his. "I will take your place if you wish to retire to your room and rest, my angel."

She snatched it away, eyes blazing. "*Rest*? No, I will make short work of this, I assure you."

She whirled away to a corner of the room and started counting aloud. The participants scrambled to leave in a flurry of laughs and squeals. Guy kept his eyes locked on Antonia. She'd opted to head for the dining room, a bold choice given that it was next to the drawing room and would give her fewer places to hide. However, that also meant that the rest of the guests had sought hiding spots in the opposite direction. Had she done this on purpose, knowing he would follow her? Whatever the case, it made what he had in mind all the easier.

He caught up with her in three long strides, reached out and grabbed her wrist. She emitted a small gasp and turned, her face flushed and radiant.

"I fear I did not think this through," she whispered. "Where shall we hide? Under the table?"

He stole a light kiss from her, then led her past the table. "I have a better idea."

Careful observation revealed what he was looking for: a door blending with the elegant paneling. He pressed on it with his palm, releasing a latch inside that allowed it to open.

Antonia gave a little laugh. "The service corridor?"

He simply smiled and motioned for her to precede him inside before closing the door behind them. The corridor was plunged in gray dimness, a simple unadorned hallway that ran parallel to the dining room, then turned sharply in what Guy supposed was the staircase leading to the kitchens.

Antonia looked around in wonder. "I never would have thought of this myself. I don't even remember seeing a door there."

"Locating the service corridors and stairwells is actually quite useful in a number of situations," Guy murmured, snaking an arm around her waist and pulling her closer. "And one situation in particular."

He brought her mouth to his and she melted against him, so tender and eager that the arousal he'd felt simmering for hours suddenly snapped loose and rushed forth with alarming speed. A rumble of thunder resonated throughout the house. The storm was right above them.

Guy pressed Antonia against the wall and let his lips trail down to her neck, laying a series of wet, open-mouthed kisses on her silky skin until her breath quickened and her hips arched against his straining erection.

"As its name indicates," he continued between kisses, his hands cupping the tantalizing curves of her backside, "it can come in handy when one has the irrepressible urge to service a woman and simply cannot wait until a bedroom is secured."

Antonia sighed, rolling her head to expose her throat to him. "Guy… If someone catches us…"

"No servants here at this hour."

"The door is unlocked. Victoire or someone else might… *Oh!*"

He gently bit into the curve of her breast, letting his teeth graze over the plump softness before tracing it with his tongue. Getting caught in the act was the least of his concerns at the moment. More to the point was how to stave off his yearning for her. If it hadn't been so short a while after her first time, he would already be taking her against the wall, hard and steady, her legs wrapped around his waist while he buried himself into that tight, drenched heat again and again. For now, a simple taste would have to do, but damn if he hadn't been thirsty for it all morning.

Another rumble of thunder. He dropped to his knees. Antonia looked down at him, eyes wide, and gave a little whimper.

"Now, love, you're going to have to be very quiet," he teased, bunching up her skirts over her legs.

"Quiet? I can't. Not when you… do those things to me and I…"

"You flatter me. But if you make the same beautiful music as this morning, it'll take but a moment for someone to discover us." He stroked her thigh, kissed the sensitive skin on the inside. "Lady's choice, of course. Shall I continue?"

Antonia pressed her lips in a thin line and nodded, holding up her skirts and giving him full access to what he craved. As soon as he put his mouth on her, she stifled a moan with her palm, but he held her firmly into place, running the tip of his tongue along the crease, flicking and sucking the tiny bud where her pleasure throbbed. Gently at first, then more boldly. She no longer showed any trace of the reservations she'd expressed that morning and thank the devil for that. She was the best thing he'd ever tasted, sweeter than a ripe peach, headier than the rarest of vintages, and he would have no qualms proving to her again and again by gorging himself on her pleasure.

He spread her thighs wider. Her legs were barely holding her up now, and her free hand dug into his shoulder while the other desperately muffled her cries. He yielded nothing. That damn door could open any moment and whoever followed would find him with his head buried between her legs, but he couldn't stop, wouldn't stop even if the sky itself fell down upon them. Her peak was gathering within her now, the first tremors of it rippling under his mouth. Keeping his hold strong, he thrust his tongue inside of her until a soft wail accompanied the quivering of her sex, and she finally relaxed in his grasp.

He delicately let go of her and stood. She slumped against the wall, chest heaving, eyes lidded, curls in disarray. Utter perfection. He had done that, brought her to this state. Their gazes met and he slowly passed his thumb over his lips.

"Delectable," he rasped, then took her hand to kiss her palm and all the delightful sounds it had held.

The thunder rolled again, though less powerfully this time. He caressed a curl from her face and tucked it behind her ear.

"Well, the storm seems to be passing. Perhaps we should—"

"No. Wait."

There was something in her gaze he'd never seen before. Desire, yes, but also a covetous determination, unbound by rules and doubts.

"I want to pleasure you as well."

Dear God, never had any words rushed with such alacrity to his cock. "Pleasure me?"

She hesitated only a moment before putting her hand on his chest, letting it trail down his waistcoat and finally grazing the waistband of his breeches, just above the bulge of his erection.

"Yes. Teach me. Show me how to touch you."

Arousal pulsed violently through his veins, roared in his ears more powerfully than booming thunder. He fumbled to unbutton his falls, then slowly guided her where she needed to go, keeping his gaze fixed on her face, his heart hammering away.

Finally, dainty fingers wrapped around his rigid staff. A groan burst forth from deep inside his chest.

"Shhh," she whispered, a small smile on her lips. "We must be quiet, remember?"

He grinned at her playfulness. Giving back as good as she got, then. That was promising indeed.

"Here," he murmured, wrapping his hand over hers. "Strengthen your grip."

"I wouldn't want to—"

"Don't be afraid of hurting me. It's what makes it pleasurable when you move... just so..."

He led her hand to the tip of his shaft, then back down again, closing his eyes against the delicious friction. Antonia continued the movement, carefully and deliberately, growing accustomed to the sensation.

"Like that?" she asked.

The angelic sweetness of her voice, even as she was stroking him with increasing vigor, was near enough to make him come on the spot. "Yes. Just like that."

She hastened her pace and his forehead fell to her shoulder, his breath tearing painfully from him, his muscles clenched to draw out the searing pleasure as long as possible. Heavens above, she was a fast learner.

"Keep going," he panted. "I'm close."

Her grip tightened and he jerked his hips forward, the tautness in his groin spiraling madly to the breaking point until his climax hurled through him in violent racks of white-hot bliss.

Spent and momentarily satiated, he retrieved a kerchief from his pocket to wipe Antonia's nimble hand clean, and she embraced him, rubbing her cheek against his temple. "How did I do?"

"Exceedingly well," he replied, struggling to catch his breath. "Though it would be in my best interest to say you need practice."

She smiled. "I wouldn't mind if you did."

He lifted his head to kiss her. "You'll be the death of me yet. But we should probably find another hiding place first." With a glance at the door, he tucked himself back into his breeches and straightened his waistcoat. "Someone's bound to come looking here at some point."

As if on cue, there was a light rap on the wall. Antonia immediately tensed, and he ran his hand down her back in a soothing motion, though his senses were on alert as well.

"*Trouvé*," came a muffled voice. "But I'll give you a minute to, erm… make yourselves presentable."

Guy let out a breath. *Nicolas*. Of course, he would guess where Guy would take Antonia. And if other guests had joined in the hunt, he'd come to find them before anyone else could catch them in the act.

"Oh God," Antonia whimpered, covering her face in embarrassment. "How much do you suppose he's heard?"

"Enough," Guy replied, unable to keep the amusement out of his voice. "But if it's any comfort, I don't think he needed to hear anything to know what we were up to."

Her hands dropped to her side, but her expression was still troubled. "He knows what mischief you're capable of, but whatever will he think of *me*?"

Guy took her hand in his. Embarrassment didn't surprise him. This, however, did. Why would Nicolas's opinion matter in the least, especially after what she'd learned about his past? For that matter, why would *anyone*'s opinion matter?

"Be easy, love, all is well. As I told you, Nicolas and I watch out for each other. Our secret is safe with him."

Antonia nodded, gaining some of her composure back. But as he led her to the door, the word lingered in his mind. *Secret.* How long would it stay that way?

He had never cared for secrets. Hated them, in fact. The need for discretion and propriety had always rankled him, and often brought him to heads with his father. Fun and games were one thing, but for the rest, he'd had enough hiding to last a lifetime.

He squeezed Antonia's hand. It was time to step out into the light, and damn what anyone would have to say about it.

Chapter Eleven

"WHAT A MARVELOUS time we had last night, mademoiselle. A shame you had to miss it."

Antonia smiled at Lisette's reflection in the mirror. The lines on her chambermaid's face were more drawn than usual, but her eyes were as lively as ever.

"I am sorry for it, yes," she replied. "But the feast itself was a success, that's all that matters. And with such pleasant weather, unlike tonight."

Drops pattered softly on the windowpane. Another storm rumbled in the far distance before the guests had retired to their rooms to get ready for the evening, bringing a fresh trail of rain behind it.

"A shame it was spoiled for Monsieur de Cazal as well, with what happened with Lenoir."

Antonia fiddled with a ribbon that lay on the dressing table. "You heard all about it, then?"

"Oh yes, mademoiselle. The footmen told us everything." She took a strand of Antonia's hair, coiled it expertly and secured it with a pin, keeping her eyes on her work. "There is not much that goes on within the walls of such a great house that doesn't make its way downstairs, and rather sooner than later."

Antonia's stomach gave a lurch. Lisette's expression remained carefully neutral, but something in the maid's choice of words alerted her. Did Lisette know about the night she'd spent in Guy's bed? Or even about the way they'd pleasured each other in the service corridor? Someone could have heard them while going up the stairs, seen them even, then turned, all too eager to share the gossip with the rest of the staff. She and Guy wouldn't have noticed, given their position. Her cheeks burned and the familiar tug of want awakened as she recalled the sight of Guy's dark head of hair moving between her legs as he licked and sucked her most intimate places, the way his full lips glistened when he pulled away, the fierce possessiveness in his gaze that made her breath catch even now.

Dear God, what was wrong with her? She should be alarmed at the idea that someone had seen them. Alarmed and chastened into taking more precautions. Her reputation could suffer greatly from this if word somehow followed her back to Chartres. And yet it did nothing to calm the insistent need exciting her senses, the relentless pressure that surged forth every time she thought of Guy. All her misgivings were replaced by one simple command: *Again.*

She felt almost sick from it, a similar sensation to eating too much honey and feeling as though it was coursing in her veins, thick and cloying. Was it the same for everyone? She glanced up at Lisette, wondering if the maid might understand her plight. If only Honorine was here to advise her as well. Before they were even married, she had confided in Antonia that she and Stanislas had gotten *carried away* behind the woodshed, resulting in the most pleasant of interludes for them both. Surely she would not begrudge Antonia getting carried away in a similar manner.

That is different, a voice in her head rebuked. *They were engaged. You are not. Guy has made no promises.*

None indeed. The only promise that existed between them had been made by their parents on their behalf, long ago. So why did it feel like her bond with Guy was stronger and more legitimate than any betrothal?

"There, all finished," Lisette said, carefully patting the artful pile of curls she had put together. "Tomorrow you must let me try this new hairstyle we spoke of, so that you may be lovelier still for the ball."

Antonia rose from her chair. "Thank you, Lisette. With pleasure."

The maid straightened her back and gave a polite smile. "I shall be waiting for you when you retire."

"That is not necessary," Antonia replied quickly. Too quickly. Blast. "Madame Rouget will no doubt insist I stay at the card table until she herself returns to her room," she explained. "With all the preparations for the ball tomorrow, it's better if you get some rest."

"That is too kind of you, *mademoiselle*."

Antonia took her shawl and fan and cast one last glance at Lisette before leaving the room, hoping to find some clue as to what she was thinking, but her expression was as placid and affable as ever.

When she arrived downstairs, Claudine was already asking for her second glass of *aperitivo*. She appeared to be in particularly high spirits for some reason, and her boisterous remarks attracted even more pained shrugs from her son.

At dinner, Antonia sat between the two of them, while Guy, who had joined the party directly in the dining room, was at the head of the table between François and Marie-Louise. Their hosts seemed to have an endless supply of questions for him about his run-in with Lenoir, and much of the conversation at the rest of the table revolved around the terrible dangers to be met in Paris and the dreadful ills of life in the capital.

"Mud and muck everywhere you step."

"Some neighborhoods are so overrun with cutthroats even the national guard dare not go there."

"Oh, and the noise at all hours, it's impossible to get a proper night of sleep!"

"A wonder, truly, that so many of you live a part of the year there," Nicolas remarked slyly, echoing her thoughts, "given that it is such a filthy, dismal place. Why not simply retire to the countryside altogether?"

This provoked a vivid response in defense of Paris, which was then portrayed in no uncertain terms as an incomparable center of culture and pleasure.

"There's never a dull evening, with all the theaters and concert halls offering entertainment. I would be bored witless living in the countryside!"

"Nowhere else are the people so enlightened and forward-thinking."

"Typical Parisians," Claudine told Antonia with a little laugh. "They will moan about how awful the city is until someone suggests they live somewhere else."

Antonia smiled in response and slipped a glance in Guy's direction. He was listening politely to the debate while sipping his wine, though his fingers were tapping the tablecloth in a restless beat. Was he as impatient as she was for dinner to be over? The back of her chair seemed stiffer, her dress and stays and chemise more cumbersome, the heat of the dining room more suffocating. She was intensely aware of everything around her, and intensely desirous to bolt from the table and out of the room.

Looking to distract herself, she let her gaze wander over the rest of the guests, only to pause on Victoire. Especially on a topic like the merits of Parisian life, such a fashionable woman, with access to the most exclusive salons, would be looked to as the voice of authority, yet her mouth was set in a stubborn pout and her eyes remained downcast. Monsieur de Brienne had taken his usual seat beside her, but he had turned away to talk with the person on his left.

Claudine leaned closer to Antonia and lowered her tone. "I see you've noticed that something is amiss between our two lovers. I will tell you what I've heard when we retire to the card room."

Antonia gave a small nod. She wasn't one to indulge in gossip, but something in the pit of her gut told her she needed to hear this. After all, hadn't Victoire been the one to make that cruel wager with Guy? What if De Brienne had found them out?

"Is everything all right, my dear?" Claudine asked. "Your face looks awfully flushed."

"Perhaps I've had a little too much wine."

"Oh my, I fear I've had a bad influence on you. Here, remember what Monsieur de Cazal said the other day? Have a glass of water and you'll feel all better."

Antonia took a long, slow drink. Mercy, when was this interminable dinner finally going to end? Thankfully, the *entremets* were brought to the table and she was soon released from her agonizing wait.

Now all she had to do was to find a way to endure the second part of the evening. But first, she let Claudine take her by the arm. After telling Baptiste to hurry along to the card room and reserve them seats at a table, she led Antonia at a slow pace, placing her fan in front of her face.

"Marie-Louise has informed me that Victoire and Xavier were heard quarreling in their room."

"Really? By whom?"

Claudine tittered. "By one of the maids, who else? It was five o'clock in the morning."

Antonia unfolded her own fan and gave it a flutter, trying to cool herself in vain. At that same hour, she and Guy had been making just as much noise—or rather, he had been coaxing desperate cries of pleasure from her that she had not thought for a moment to contain. She pushed the thought from her mind and turned to Claudine.

"What were they arguing about?"

"Well, apparently Xavier accused Victoire of tiring of him and wanting to take another lover. Which isn't surprising in the least, because she's never been known to stay with a man for more than a few months before getting bored and seeking a better offer."

Antonia frowned. "A better offer?"

"Someone who will pay her gambling debts, buy her dresses, keep her in the lifestyle to which she is accustomed. Monsieur Le Plessis Tailland, her husband, regularly cuts her off when her spending grows too extravagant."

Her mouth suddenly turned dry. This was the woman whose favor Guy had been seeking not two weeks past. He had told her he no longer cared about her, but still…

"Xavier has been most generous in that regard," Claudine continued. "Well, he can afford it, given his family's vast fortune. But here's the rub: according to my sources, Xavier believes Victoire means to sate her lust with another suitor while keeping *him* at hand to loosen his purse strings."

"Do you think he's right?"

Claudine gave a wry smile. "I do not doubt for a second that he is. Victoire's appetites are many, and as of yet she has never been given a reason to moderate them."

They had arrived in the card room and took their seat next to Baptiste, who had enlisted Marie-Louise to be the fourth player at pinochle. Antonia did not know what to make of what Claudine had told her. De Brienne had said nothing about the wager or Guy in particular, but she remained unsettled by this turn of events. Unsettled, and in desperate need to be alone with Guy, to reassure herself in the knowledge that what had passed between them wasn't just a temporary distraction from a bigger prize. To forget about everything else in the strong, solid warmth of his arms.

"I feel I will get lucky this evening," Baptiste exclaimed as he dealt the cards.

"Not if I can help it, my darling boy," Claudine replied. "I am ready to go on all night if that's what it takes to beat you."

Antonia suppressed a groan. This evening might not turn out quite as she had planned. How could she beg off and claim to be tired after supposedly sleeping for so long the previous evening? Besides, it was bad form to leave the table now. During the *aperitivo*, Baptiste had gone on at length on why four-handed pinochle was infinitely superior to other versions of the game.

She glanced at her cards and sighed. A terrible hand, as it turned out, one she played without enthusiasm, waiting for the next round with equal dismay.

"Pardon me for interrupting, but would you care to make room for me at your table?"

Her eyes met a lime green waistcoat before traveling upward to Nicolas's smiling face.

"Why, Monsieur Lefevre, you are most welcome to join us," Claudine said, batting her eyelashes as quickly as her fan.

Baptiste rolled his eyes heavenwards. "*Maman*, as you well know, there is no such thing as five-handed pinochle. No offense to you, Monsieur Lefevre, but perhaps there is another table looking for a player?"

"Indeed," Nicolas said with a little sigh, "though none so enticing as this one."

Marie-Louise and Claudine both erupted in giggles and Nicolas's smile widened. For a second, he caught Antonia's gaze, and the complicity she saw there made everything clear.

"Oh, well... Monsieur Lefevre may take my place," she offered. "I think I'll go to the music room and listen in if anyone takes a turn at the piano."

"Are you certain, my dear?" Claudine asked, though with less insistence than she had shown before.

"Please. Enjoy your game. Perhaps I will join you again later."

With any luck, Nicolas's charming antics would make Claudine and Marie-Louise forget about her, and Baptiste would be too engrossed in his game to wonder where she was. She hurried out of the card room, then up the stairs. If Guy had arranged for Nicolas to give her a means of escaping, he would certainly come to her room; they had both agreed it would be more convenient, as a man wandering the corridors at dawn would attract fewer unwanted questions than a young lady.

Just as she was about to reach her door, a hand grabbed her arm and she was pulled against a hard, familiar heat, and surrounded by the scent of fresh grass after a rain shower.

"Guy," she murmured, but his lips came down on hers before she could say another word.

Several long, searing, breathless moments later, they finally broke apart, but Guy refused to let her go so she could open the door. "I have been waiting all day for this. I cannot bear another second when you are not in my arms."

"You silly man, it will only take a moment," she laughed. "Would you not rather enjoy the softness of my bed?"

He finally released her, a dark strand of hair falling on his forehead and giving him a raffish mien. "I would, though as you well know by now, I make do with any location."

Her pulse quickened and a new kind of urgency surged through her. Yes, another second would be unbearable. She took his hand and led him inside her room, carefully locking the door behind her.

DAWN ONCE AGAIN found them in bed together, though this time they had not wasted the hours in slumber. Antonia was light-headed from lack of sleep, deliciously sore, aware of places inside her body she had not known existed, and ways for Guy to reach that deep, delicious spot that she could never have suspected.

If anyone had told her that a man could turn a woman over and join their bodies together from behind, she would have thought it brutal and bestial, no more appealing than what went on between cattle in a field. Yet when Guy had rolled her on her stomach, spreading her legs and gripping her hips to thrust slowly into her, the sensation had made her head spin and her lips part in a series of breathy cries.

After that, there wasn't anything she didn't want to try.

"Will you not place yourself on top of me this time?" Guy asked her after they'd woken up from a short slumber, kissing her neck and pushing her mussed hair back from her face.

"Me on top? Is that pleasurable for you?" she replied breathlessly.

He grinned. "You should know by now there aren't many things that are not pleasurable for me when you are naked in my bed. Here, let me show you."

He rose to sit on the mattress and pulled her up. She slid her hand up his thigh and cupped his aroused member, moving her hand up and down, relishing in the hot, heavy feel of him against her hand.

"Easy, love," he groaned. "Or I will not last long enough. Come, are you ready for me?"

A renewed flush of heat had pooled between her thighs. How could she want him so inexhaustibly still after spending the entire night in his arms? "I feel I will always be ready for you," she breathed.

"Music to my ears," he replied, and guided her into position so that she straddled him, her breasts pressing against his chest.

He took his manhood in hand and ran the tip of it over her crease, making her whimper with need. "Ah yes, you *are* ready. Weeping for me. Eager little thing, aren't you?" He pressed a bit harder, just at her entrance, and smiled as her whimpers grew louder. "Lower yourself onto me."

She took him in slowly and he gave a low groan, thrusting up the rest of the way to bury himself to the hilt. His hands gripped her hips to roll them forward and increase the intimate friction of their bodies while he jerked deep inside her.

"Do you feel that? How well you take me when you are on top of me?"

She nodded desperately, her senses in a frenzy. Guy grasped her buttocks and surged forth, hitting a spot so exquisitely sensitive she thought she might reach her peak at that very moment. Her gasp turned into a low moan.

"That's it," he growled. "Take me deeper. Take all of me now."

His hands incited her to increase her pace and she threw her head back, leaving him free to suckle her breasts. She was burning, melting, her entire being consumed with such intense pleasure that she no longer knew who she was. There was only this, only him, only them.

"Guy…"

"God, when you say my name like that…" His arms came around her to hold her steady and he pounded roughly within her, giving her everything. "Again."

"*Guy*. Guy, please…"

"I will never get enough of this. Of you. Never." His eyes searched for hers. "Tell me how much you need this."

Whatever he desired, he could have. Anything, as long as he didn't stop. "Yes, yes, I need this, I need you inside of me," she mewled. "Keep going, I beg of you, it's too good…"

He thrust deeper still, and a surge of ecstasy jolted through her body. She clamped her hand over her mouth to stifle a scream, but he tore it away.

"None of that. Let me hear your pleasure."

And so she did, crying out with the force of her climax. Guy's thrusts increased until he lifted her, abruptly pulling away and spilling his seed onto her stomach as he groaned against her neck. But his arms did not slacken, nor did he draw back entirely to clean her with the sheet. Instead, he simply looked at her, from the juncture of her thighs to her face, slowly and languorously, as if overwhelmed by the sight of her.

"Come to Paris with me," he breathed.

Still reeling from the onslaught of pleasure that had swept over her, she tried to make sense of what he had just said. She must not have heard him correctly. "What?"

"Leave with me tomorrow. Come to Paris."

She untangled herself from him, sitting on the rumpled bed, her mind still refusing to believe his words. "I don't understand.

Come to Paris? I… You can't be serious."

His eyes squeezed shut for a moment, as if he were in pain, but then they were right back on her, a blue fire that burned with unabated intensity. "Antonia. Please. Don't think, just—"

Before he could finish his sentence, a loud crash resounded just in front of the door. Antonia gave a little cry and instinctively brought the sheets up to cover herself, but Guy simply turned, his body tense and ready to spring into action.

"What the devil are you doing here?" cried a feminine voice. "Look what you made me do!"

Antonia's eyes widened. "It's Lisette," she whispered.

"Not my fault you dropped the pitcher," a coarser feminine voice replied.

"Not your fault? And I suppose it's not your fault either you had your ear pressed against the door, listening in on my mistress? Now get out of here!" There was a long moment of silence, then Lisette continued, talking to herself out loud. "I suppose I should clean this up and get another pitcher of water."

Antonia brought her knees up her chest and curled up against them. It was obvious that Lisette was not only talking to herself, but to them, to let them know that Guy had just enough time to slip out before she returned. She had been looking out for them.

"Damnation," Guy grumbled. "If I catch whoever was eaves-dropping…"

Antonia raised her head to look at him. "Forget the servant. Why do you think she was there? Certainly someone must have sent her for the sole purpose of compromising us."

Guy's mouth tightened into a grim line. "Yes. Someone."

With a sinking feeling, she realized they were thinking of the same person, and had no need to speak her name.

"I should dress and go back to my room," Guy said, rising from the bed. "It's probably better if we're not seen together today. No use raising even more suspicions."

"Yes. Of course."

He was right. It was logical. Why give Victoire more ammunition against them if she meant to cause trouble? Yet she couldn't help but wonder if it was also a way to flee from what he had asked her, to avoid her questions.

And this time, she had no desire to hold him back, for her own answers eluded her.

Chapter Twelve

GUY TAPPED HIS finger against the rim of his empty plate. The morning room was still empty save for him and two footmen, standing still and solemn while the rest of the chateau bustled with preparations for the ball.

Try as he might, he couldn't rid himself of the nagging sense of dread that had seized him when they'd heard Victoire's maid outside their door. It had to be her. No one else would contrive such a vile, shameless plan in order to compromise them.

Yet what would have happened if they hadn't been interrupted?

He stood and slapped his gloves against his thigh. By God, what a fool he'd been to ask her to come with him. Antonia was right. It didn't make sense.

But remembering the heights of pleasure she'd brought him to, recalling with perfect clarity her supple body entwined with his, her face flushed with her own climax, the seed he had spilled on the soft plane of her stomach, he couldn't bring himself to regret his words. He didn't want to give her up. He didn't want to leave for Paris without her.

The solution was glaringly obvious: make good on their parents' original intentions and ask Antonia to marry him. But simply thinking the words made his gut churn and his heart race with savage, uncontrollable panic.

He needed to ride this off, clear his head. Just as he was about to leave the morning room, Nicolas entered, his face drawn and his hair disheveled.

"Rough night?" Guy greeted him, then noticed his friend wasn't wearing a cravat and had on the same waistcoat as the previous evening, something Nicolas had once described as the first warning sign of the imminent collapse of civilized society. "*Very* rough. Good Lord, man, you look like you slept in your clothes."

"I did," Nicolas grunted. "I was too exhausted to take them off again when I returned to my room."

"*Again?*"

Guy raised an eyebrow, but Nicolas simply gave a wide yawn, then went to take two brioche rolls from the table. "Let us step outside for the remainder of our conversation. I take it you're going riding? I'll walk you to the stables."

"Protecting the lady's honor?"

"No. Rather her son's delicate sensibilities if he should happen to hear us."

Guy shook his head and bit back a laugh. He could only hope Rouget's obliviousness had shielded him from the worst of it. "Is that a first for you? Making off with the mother under her son's nose? I can't recall if you ever pulled off that particular exploit in my company."

"I think so, yes. Oh, wait." He frowned, as if searching his memory. "Yes, definitely a first."

As soon they were outside, Nicolas bit into one of the rolls and devoured the mouthful as if he hadn't eaten in days.

"How you have enough energy to saddle a horse and go for a jaunt in the countryside is beyond me," he said through a mouthful of bread. "Unless you fell asleep after one go and spent the rest of the night snoring in your *demoiselle*'s arms."

"Far from it," Guy replied with a grin. "By the way, I should thank you for your admirable deflection skills last night."

"Think nothing of it. Claudine was particularly receptive to my charms. Loudly, inexhaustibly receptive."

"I can't say I'm surprised, after you *accidentally* ended up hiding with her behind the curtains of the music room and getting a handful of something you shouldn't. Though when I asked you to distract her I rather thought it would more of the same playful mischief, and not… whatever it was that left you in such a state."

Nicolas gulped down the last of the rolls. "Bit of friendly advice, if you ever need to exercise your endurance, a merry widow is worth a few rounds of *savate*. You see, this is why I value experience above all else: complete lack of inhibition. That, and avoiding other complications that may arise with a more… delicate partner."

Guy halted in the middle of the lane leading to the stables. Something in Nicolas's shrewd gaze cut through his temporary cheer rending it like so much sheer cloth. "What are you implying?"

"Come, now. You cannot tell me you are planning on letting Antonia leave tomorrow after shaking her hand and telling her Godspeed."

His tone was softer, almost compassionate. Guy had only heard it once before, when Nicolas had helped him up from the dirtied pavement, that night in Palais Royal.

"What if I am?" he retorted.

Nicolas observed him for a moment before pursuing. "It would be no small feat of hypocrisy for me to deny the right of two willing adults to indulge in mutual pleasure, so long as no undue promises are made and both are clear on their feelings. If this is the case between you and Antonia, by all means, proceed as you wish. If not—"

"I never promised her anything."

Factually true. In essence, a bold-faced lie. Every caress and kiss and smile they had shared was a promise. A vow. If he married her…

He would have to protect her. Cherish her. Build a family and a future.

And do all of this while knowing that in the blink of an eye, it could come crashing down. He could fail her, fail their children, fail to avoid separation and suffering and death. One single whoosh of a blade coming down upon his neck…

He loosened his cravat, nearly gasping for air. "I must go," he muttered, and stalked off toward the stables, leaving Nicolas in the middle of the path.

Once he had saddled and mounted his horse, his nerves settled somewhat. Being out in the open countryside was a relief, an escape from the trap he had set himself. He started up a familiar road, a long, gentle slope wide and level enough to build up some speed before reaching the top of a low hill. He galloped onward, then stopped, finding some measure of serenity in the landscape only to have it shattered by the thundering of hooves.

He glanced over his shoulder. *Victoire.* Hot anger seized his chest. She was wearing an elegant riding outfit in a striking yellow color, and her form was graceful and controlled. Perfect, really. His anger swelled when he thought of Antonia that morning, her hair mussed from their lovemaking, clutching the rumpled sheet to her chest while her eyes filled with shame and dismay at being caught.

Damnation, he needed to get a hold of himself. He straightened his back and turned his horse to meet her head-on. Might as well get this over with.

Victoire slowed to a trot as she approached, then stopped her mount a few meters away.

"*Madame,*" he said in a clipped tone.

Victoire merely laughed. "My goodness, aren't we formal this morning?"

"I fail to see why you would want it otherwise."

Her dark eyes glinted with amusement but it was flat, joyless somehow. "How quickly one forgets. Have you decided to turn a new leaf entirely, *monsieur*? Or have you just changed your mind regarding our arrangement?"

Guy clenched his jaw and glared at her. He didn't owe her an explanation. He didn't owe her a damn thing.

"I've heard whisperings that you have completed your side of the bargain," she continued with a smile. "It's only natural that I would ask whether you wished for mine to go ahead as well."

"Stop it."

She gestured toward a nearby thicket. "Nothing easier than to tie the reins of our horses and enjoy some privacy."

"I said, *stop it.*"

Something in his gaze made her smile wither. "Just as I thought. You're nothing but a weak, besotted fool fancying himself in love with that simpering chit."

He gripped the reins. His horse pawed the ground nervously. But Victoire wasn't done.

"Unless you are even more perverse than I thought and are simply intent on ruining her more thoroughly before you tire of her? After all, if you had cast her off immediately as you planned, you would have spared her a great deal of pain."

"Is that a threat?" he snarled.

She lifted her chin. "You have despoiled her all on your own already. Now that she's a part of our world, she will have to play by our rules."

She turned away before he could answer and spurred her horse into a canter. Just as well. He didn't know how long he would have lasted before his control slipped and he gave in to the urge to grab her arm, shake her, scare her enough to permanently wipe the smile off her face. The anger abated somewhat, but still a tight knot gripped his stomach and made his muscles tense.

The rest of the day and the evening stretched before him, deprived of the comfort and relief he found in Antonia's arms, loaded with the burden of figuring out what in devil's name he was going to do now. He looked toward the horizon again, fighting the urge to gallop mindlessly until he'd outrun his thoughts.

THE BALLROOM WINDOWS had been opened wide to let in the cool, grass-scented night air, but little of it seemed to make it past the sill. Antonia fanned herself, watching as the crowd of guests twirled on the parquet floor to a lively waltz.

Next to her, Claudine yawned behind her fan. She was uncharacteristically sedate that evening, despite having napped all afternoon, as if all her lively energy had been drained.

"Forgive me," she told Antonia. "It's so dreadfully stuffy in here. Why did Marie-Louise feel the need to invite so many people? One cannot fit all the local bigwigs into such a small ballroom. The original party alone would have made a crush."

"If you invite one of them, you have to invite them all," Antonia replied, amused at her huffiness. "I know how it is in Chartres. Not that my parents ever threw a ball such as this one, but people are all too happy to gossip."

And they could be merciless, especially when it came to a woman's reputation. She slipped a glance toward Guy, who was standing a few meters away. They had barely exchanged a word all day, but this evening he was never far from her, always within sight. And Victoire, thankfully, was lost somewhere on the other side of the room, though Antonia had caught a few glimpses of her vivid turquoise gown.

She sighed. Sooner or later, she would have to talk to Guy. And he would have to repeat, or take back, what he had asked her that morning. Hours had passed, and she was no closer to an answer.

"At last!" Baptiste made his way toward them, two glasses of lemonade in hand, a crimson flush on his cheeks. "Good God, what a crush. Took me half an hour just to get to the table."

"I suppose they're going all out before we all leave tomorrow," Claudine said, then clinked her glass with Antonia's. "I'll be happy to be home, but I will miss you terribly, my dear."

Her words pinched Antonia's heart. She had been so preoc-cupied with Guy's offer that she hadn't even stopped to consider that she and Claudine were about to part ways. In little less than two weeks, she had become a true, trustworthy friend.

Trustworthy enough to confide in, even now. Antonia bit her lower lip. If only she could find the courage to tell her and seek her advice…

"Oh, listen, they're playing another one," Baptiste suddenly exclaimed as the violin ensemble struck a new waltz. "Would you be so kind as to grant me this dance, Mademoiselle Saint Yves?"

Antonia smiled. "Yes, of course."

She desperately needed the distraction. Claudine took her glass and she followed Baptiste to the floor. Guy wasn't dancing. In fact, he hadn't danced all evening. She couldn't help but look his away again. Lord, would her heart ever stop fluttering every time she laid eyes on him? Though the blue jacket he usually wore complimented the stunning color of his eyes, he was breathtakingly handsome in his formal black attire. His brow was furrowed and his gaze seemed lost somewhere far away in the distance.

Her stomach tied in a painful knot. Was he thinking about what he'd told her? Regretting it, even?

In an attempt to drive the maddening doubts from her mind, she turned her attention back to Baptiste and he whirled her into a turn. Yet with each turn she could hear the words echoing in her head, in time with the music. *Come with me. Come with me. Come with me.*

She couldn't. It was madness. What would she tell Honorine? And Jerome? When he learned of it, her brother would hunt Guy down and murder him. And blame Honorine for the entire ordeal, since she had been the one to encourage Antonia to accept the Aubertine's invitation.

Besides, what on earth would she do in Paris, besides being with Guy?

Come with me. Come with me. Come with me.

Being with Guy… Wasn't that enough, after waiting all these years? Would she simply give up on making her own way in life and retreat to the safety of what she'd always known? Her family. Her home. A place of comfort, yes, but what if she woke up years from now, filled with regret at not having taken this risk?

"What an enjoyable evening, is it not?"

Looking up at Baptiste's rosy cheeks and pleasant smile, she almost wanted to scream in frustration. This was the type of man Honorine had meant for her to meet. If only she had played her cards right… If only she had resolved to encourage his attentions…

If only she didn't love Guy. Madly and irrevocably. Because that was the one condition that made all other choices impossible. Leaving him would be like tearing her own heart out.

Her head was spinning, her breath short. The chords of the waltz cut through her like blades.

Baptiste slowed. "Are you all right?"

"Forgive me, I… I need to rest a bit."

"Of course."

He led her to the other side of the ballroom, then helped her to a bench and stood beside her awkwardly.

"I shall go retrieve your glass of lemonade. Maybe it'll help restore your spirits."

"Yes, thank you," she murmured.

After a few moments, she started to breathe more easily and stood up. She should leave the ballroom altogether. It would be impolite of her to retreat to her room now, but perhaps a stroll outside…

A flash of turquoise caught her eye.

"Mademoiselle Saint Yves."

Her throat tightened. This was bound to happen sooner or later. But she wasn't going to back down and scuttle away like a mouse.

She turned to see Victoire looking at her with a sweet smile, like a carnivorous flower enticing a prey. She tilted her head gracefully, and her stunning necklace of diamonds and amethysts caught the light of the chandeliers. "My, what a charming dress you're wearing. Although white may be a bold choice given the circumstances."

Antonia straightened. Her fingers tightened around her fan. "I beg your pardon?"

"Truly, I bear you no ill will. On the contrary, I wish to help you."

The condescending tone sent a bolt of anger through her. "Your help is by no means required."

Victoire's gaze flitted toward Antonia's hair, which Lisette had so carefully arranged and tied with the silver cords she'd bought. "Are you certain? You could do very well in the capital, you know, with your face and figure, but you will need some advice if you want to climb up the rungs of society."

Don't blush. Don't let yourself be shamed. She is only trying to provoke you. "I've no idea what you're talking about."

"Monsieur de Cazal invited you to join him, did he not?"

She shouldn't have been surprised. God only knew what her spy had heard. Still, she was reminded of Victoire smoothly taking the bow, pulling back the arrow, and shooting it right in the center of the target.

"That's none of your business," she retorted.

"Oh, you poor dear. In Paris, it's everyone's business."

And indeed, their conversation was starting to attract attention from several guests around them. The urge to flee made her heart thump against her chest, but she used her anger to push it back. *No. I will not run away from this. I will not be treated like a witless child.*

"If you're looking for respectability and discretion," Victoire continued, "you would be better off saddling yourself with Monsieur Rouget. Though I'm not certain such a nice boy would accept spoiled goods."

The slap struck Victoire's cheek before Antonia fully realized what she was doing. There was only fury now, red and crackling and stoked with humiliation. She thought she heard gasps. The music echoed far, far away.

"How dare you?"

Victoire touched her cheek. Disbelief turned to pure loathing. "How dare I tell the truth?" she cried as a crowd gathered around them. "You stupid little bitch. Will you try and deny that Monsieur de Cazal has offered to set you up as his mistress?"

Chapter Thirteen

"WHAT DO YOU say, de Cazal? Zephyr is quite a fine beast, isn't he?"

Guy eyed the dancers spinning and swaying in time with the waltz, looking for a mass of titian curls. Why had so many women chosen to wear white this evening?

"To allay such speed and sturdiness is rare, though I'm afraid he's a bit too spirited for me."

Finally, he spotted her, twirling in Rouget's arms. A burst of jealousy gave way to relief. As long as Antonia was dancing with that simpleton, he knew she was safe and accounted for.

He turned back to François, who was looking at him expectantly. "Forgive me. You were saying?"

"Zephyr. You've been riding him nearly every day, surely you can see his potential. With a young, steady-handed master…"

Rouget appeared in his line of sight. Alone. Blast, where had Antonia gone? The flurry of black jackets and colorful frocks made it impossible to find her.

"I'd be more than willing to consider any offer…"

The waltz stopped and the dancers cleared the floor. Antonia was on the other side of the ballroom.

So was Victoire. Damnation.

"Pardon me," he muttered, and left before François could

even finish his sentence.

The violins sounded the first few notes of a quadrille and the dancers lined up again. Guy fought his way through the crowd, heart thumping hard, but Victoire had already approached Antonia, and people were gathering around them, like blood-thirsty spectators at a *savate* match.

Or an execution.

At long last, he reached them, just in time for Victoire's words to hit him like a fist to the jaw.

"…stupid little bitch. Will you try and deny that Monsieur de Cazal has offered to set you up as his mistress?"

Too late. But perhaps there was still time to avoid the worst.

"That is *enough*," he roared, stepping forward. "Whatever you have implied, *madame*, take it back immediately."

"The kitten has claws," Victoire retorted, undeterred. "Let her answer."

He turned to Antonia. Victoire's reddened cheek left no doubt as to what had just happened, but Antonia's pale face and wide, fearful eyes made it look as if she was the one who had just been slapped. He wanted to shield her. Whisk her away. Wake both of them up from this waking nightmare.

But in spite of her distress, Antonia hadn't stepped back an inch. She could've turned back and fled. She was holding her ground. Lifting her chin.

"Guy has indeed invited me to come to Paris," she said. "Until his father's affairs are sorted and he can return to Chartres…"

His stomach plummeted. Victoire's laugh cut through him like shards of glass. "*His father's affairs?* Is that what he told you?"

The crowd of guests around them had thickened. They were now drawing more attention than the waltz or the buffet. Guy caught a glimpse of Marie-Louise on his left, and not far behind, Claudine struggling her way toward Antonia.

"Stop this immediately, Victoire," he growled in warning.

"You're the one who should apologize. First, wagering on your capacity to seduce her—"

"*Seigneur!*" Marie-Louise exclaimed.

"—then lying to her about the real reason you stayed in Paris. You retrieved your father's assets months ago, did you not? There is nothing keeping you there but the pleasures you indulge in nightly with far more beautiful women than her."

Antonia refused to look at Victoire. Refused to look at him. Her mouth opened, but no response emerged, as if a deep, acute anguish clogged her throat, and she stumbled backward.

Claudine broke through the crowd and rushed to Antonia's side. She held her by the arm and shot a look of undisguised contempt at Victoire, laced with the same pity one might reserve for a starving dog on the side of the road. "Come along now, my dear," she told Antonia. "Let us retire to a quieter place so you can sit down and breathe."

He needed to follow her. He was frozen in place. No, he must do something, *anything*. His body finally heeded the impulse to stalk them through the crowd, but a firm hand landed on his shoulder.

"Leave her be, man. She needs time to make sense of what she's just heard, and in your state you would do more harm than good."

When had Nicolas gotten here? Had he heard everything? No matter. Guy ripped free of his grip. "I *must*."

The sight of De Brienne, his lips pursed in displeasure as if he had just eaten a lemon, drew him up short. Victoire stood next to him, fanning herself languidly, basking in her own triumph.

"This is what arouses you, is it not, *madame*?" Guy thundered. Victoire startled and her smile lost some of its smugness. "Not gambling. Not fucking." Indignant gasps accompanied his words, but he barreled on. "Manipulating and destroying people, just because you can. It's no wonder you made that wager with me, offering yourself up as the prize. Lust had nothing to do with it, or you would have found your way to my bed easily enough."

Victoire blanched. De Brienne, on the other hand, didn't move an inch, and remained silent.

"I'll meet you at dawn if you feel so inclined, *monsieur*," Guy told him. "Though I daresay she's not worth the price of the powder you'll put in your pistol."

He stalked away amid a sea of murmurs. Devil take all these hypocrites. They had had their evening's entertainment.

He found Claudine and Antonia in the sitting room, huddling together on the divan in the dim light of the chandeliers. Claudine had her arm around Antonia's shoulders, but Antonia was curiously still. Despondent. As if she couldn't even muster up enough energy to cry.

"I wish to speak to Antonia in private," he said.

Claudine looked up at him, for all the world looking like a mother who was about to give her child the scolding of a lifetime. "*Monsieur*, I think it is best if you—"

"Please, Claudine," Antonia let out in a resigned murmur. "Leave us for a moment."

Claudine bit her lip and hesitated before rising from the divan. As she made her way out, she cast one last look that was decidedly more threatening than motherly at Guy, then closed the door.

Heavy silence settled over them. The chandeliers cast an almost eerie glow on the delicately ornate furniture, the shiny silk upholstery, the fine porcelain vases. Guy was overwhelmed by the absurdity of it all. What was the point in creating and displaying all these pretty things, when one knew how easily they could be destroyed?

"Is it true, then? Did you manage to retrieve everything that belonged to your father?"

His gaze met Antonia's. Her face was impassive, but her gray eyes were two pools of agony. He clenched his jaw and nodded.

"And yet Lazare Fournier assured us that you hadn't—"

"That's none of his concern," he snapped. "Neither is it yours."

"He was your father's assistant," she countered. "He's trying to get the bank up and running again. How is it not his business?

You *lied* to him."

The bank, the assets, the business. Why did she even care about any of it? His father had cared as well, much more than he ever had about his own son. And Guy was weary to the bone of coming second. "Enough about the damn bank. That's not the issue."

"You're right. It's not. So tell me why you're staying in Paris. Why you haven't come back." Her voice wavered. "Why you asked me to join you there."

If only he could take back what he had said... or what he had done with her... But he didn't want to. Worse, he didn't want to apologize for it. "I asked you to join me because... because..."

"You want me to be your mistress."

Coming from her mouth instead of Victoire's, the word sounded ten times worse. "No, I never said that."

"You want me to share your bed and stay in your home without any official status of my own. That is a mistress."

Her reasoning was logical, but still anger surged through him. How could she believe him to be so calculating? He had asked her in all sincerity, in a moment of sheer vulnerability, yet she made it sound like he had deceived her. "I asked you to come with me. No more, no less. If you are angry because I failed to make an offer of marriage like a proper gentleman..."

She stood, two spots of red appearing on her cheeks. "Do not make this sound like I'm trying to wheedle a proposal from you," she flared. "If I wanted propriety and honor, I would not have let you take me to bed. I am angry because you're not giving me a proper reason why you would avoid marriage. Why you're staying in the capital instead of returning home. Why you're pretending to be a *débauché* when you are quite clearly nothing of the sort."

He stared at her, stunned by the onslaught of truths she had unleashed on him. And she would not stop until he himself gave her truth in return. Blood pounded in his skull, and the walls of the room seemed to narrow.

"You're not telling me everything," she continued. "You've been hiding in Paris, and you're hiding now."

She didn't have to say the rest. He heard it loud and clear: *Coward.* A wave of fury rose within him.

"Hiding, yes, that's what we did for years, in case you'd forgotten," he shot back. "Struggling to make ends meet, working like dogs in a country that only tolerated our presence. Doing what it took to survive. I'm *still* doing what I can to survive. There's no shame in that."

"There is when you give up living in order to survive."

"*Living.*" He gave a joyless laugh. "You mean settling down in a house, producing children and being an honest citizen? All the things we are told will save us from degradation and dishonor? That is not living. That's obediently waiting for death."

She shook her head. "You don't mean that. Anyone who says that is less than a man."

Such inane, romantic notions. If she wanted the truth, then he would give it to her, in all its ugly, bloody glory.

"Really? My own father said something similar, just before my mother and I left."

She frowned. "Your father?"

"Yes. *If I go with you, I might survive, but I'll be less than a man,* or some such drivel."

"He didn't come with you to Switzerland?"

A lantern swinging on the carriage as the horses pawed with impatience. Bundles of clothing hastily gathered. His mother's pleading voice, swept away into the night by the wind. Guy could see it all so clearly, even now. *Will you not come with us, then? How are we to survive this alone?*

Joseph de Cazal had not bent. His heart must have been made of stone rather than flesh, or he simply had none. The way his mother had begged… And yet his father had sent them off with only a muttered promise to join them soon.

Damn him. Damn him to *hell.* He crossed the room, his limbs coursing with savage energy, his chest nearly bursting with rage.

"He believed that it was cowardly to abandon France, that he should stay and fight for his rights as a citizen. He didn't want to lose the business he'd worked so hard to build. So instead he lost his head."

Antonia's eyes widened and her voice came out in a trembling whisper. "What?"

"Do you think they ask animals if they want to live before they're slaughtered? Because I guarantee you, no one put the question to my father before they laid him out before *the fucking guillotine.*"

The roars of the crowd. The flash of the blade. Blood. His father's empty eyes, grimacing mouth, head tumbling down…

He picked up a bisque vase on the console next to him and smashed it against the wall.

"Guy."

He whipped around. Antonia's eyes were filled with tears, and she was shaking like a spring leaf in a storm.

He'd frightened her. He had never hated himself more. If he burned whatever bridge remained between them, it would be a small mercy.

"Honor. Marriage. Love," he said in a cold, empty voice. "I've seen where it leads. I only heard about my father's execution when someone sent us a letter informing us that he'd been condemned as a traitor to the Republic by the Revolutionary Tribunal. I was left to picture the rest for myself. But I was witness to my mother slowly drowning her grief in a sea of laudanum."

"I can't imagine…"

"No. You can't." Nor would he wish her to. By the time she had expired, Marguerite had wasted to little more than a breathing corpse. "Trust me, there is nothing romantic about dying for love. Nothing to be gained by being honorable. My parents were fools, both of them. And I'll be damned before I walk in their steps or fulfill a promise they made years ago."

Antonia closed her eyes. The tears spilled down her cheeks.

"You would… You would make us both miserable, simply because of that *wretched* betrothal."

"I have made an offer to you. The only one you're going to get. You declined it. There is nothing more to say."

She wiped her tears away and glared at him. Her beaten expression, her sorrowful eyes, her mouth set in a grim line gutted him like a sword to the stomach.

He had done that. He alone. Antonia was there, warm and giving and alive, beautiful even in her misery, and he had just severed the last thread that connected them, smashed her hopes as surely as he had the pretty bisque vase that laid in pieces on the floor.

She was right. This was not living. This was hanging on by the fingernails to a meaningless shell of existence. But it was either that, or risk plunging headfirst into the abyss.

"I see," she said, and picked up her shawl and fan. Was this truly the same woman he had held in his arms that very morning, responding so passionately to his touch? The very notion tore him in half. "Consider our acquaintance at an end, then. I wish you well, *monsieur*."

He couldn't reply. Couldn't hold her back. But as soon as she left the room, he realized he had already hit rock bottom.

Chapter Fourteen

Antonia sat at the small writing desk in her room, scribbling a few words with a shaky hand. Her head was heavy, her eyes weary from having shed so many tears during the night, between bouts of fitful sleep. Maybe she'd be able to rest in the carriage taking them home to Chartres, but in any case, distance would be a greater relief than sleep.

Behind her, Lisette packed her clothes in silence. When Antonia had returned to her room the previous evening, it had taken but one glance for her maid to guess what had happened, and she would have no doubt heard the rest from the other domestics by now.

Scandal. Seduction. Two things Antonia thought would never happen to her. Docile, discreet little Toinette, who liked novels and moonlit gardens. Toinette who was thrilled when Guy de Cazal finally looked her way and decided he wanted her in his bed. Toinette who had hoped, this time, that things would be different, that her romantic fantasies of true love would come true.

Fresh tears welled in her eyes and she stilled her quill. Foolish, naive Toinette. She felt like reaching into herself and ripping out her heart, squashing the part of her that had remained stubbornly, stupidly in love with Guy for years, that refused to grow up and listen to reason.

Well, now was the perfect moment to start. Guy had given her all the ammunition she needed to smother whatever remained of her adolescent delusions.

I have made an offer to you. The only one you're going to get.

Had she been a coward not to take it? Had she missed her chance? At this very hour, she could have been packing to join him, knowing that she would spend every night in his arms and every day in his company.

But how long before the torment caused by his parents' death caught up with them, and made him destroy whatever they would have built together?

She brushed her tears away with the back of her hand and set about finishing her letter. It was a note of thanks to Marie-Louise and François; Lisette had arranged for the carriage to come early and by the time they woke up, Antonia would most likely be gone.

Please accept my heartfelt thanks for a most wonderful stay in your company...

Empty words after last night's events. But she couldn't simply leave Verneuil without expressing gratitude toward the Aubertins.

"Here," she told Lisette when she was done. "Can you make sure the *majordome* gives this to our hosts? Oh, and ask Claudine's maid to wake her. I promised I wouldn't leave without saying goodbye."

"Very well, *mademoiselle*. I've finished packing our things, so we should be off before the hour is done."

Indeed, a short while later, Antonia found herself in the same traveling clothes she'd been wearing when she'd arrived. The ones Guy had seen her in, when they'd met in the entrance hall. A lifetime ago, it seemed.

The carriage and driver were waiting in the paved courtyard of the chateau, and Lisette was already sitting inside. Nothing to it. It was time to go.

"Antonia! Wait a moment, my dear!"

She turned around to find Claudine, her hair disheveled and clutching a peignoir against her chest over a nightrail. Antonia smiled. Irreverent to the very end.

"I'm sorry, I had the most dreadful time waking up this morning," Claudine told her. "My maid was aghast when I refused to take the time to dress, but I simply couldn't risk having you leave without saying goodbye."

Claudine paused. Was she to say more? They hadn't spoken the night before after Antonia had left the sitting room; she had gone directly to her room, too distraught to talk to anyone. What was left to say, after all? She wasn't the first woman to have been seduced by a man only to be spurned.

Antonia took Claudine's hand in hers. "That is very kind of you."

"You will write to me, won't you, my dear?"

"Of course. You have been... as true a friend as one could hope for. Especially when..."

Lord in heaven, how was it possible that she had any tears left to shed? But still they came, blurring her vision and making her tired eyes sting. Claudine embraced her, stroking her hair in a soothing motion.

"I am sorry," Antonia said, her voice muffled against Claudine's shoulder. "I... If only I had been less foolish. I know you were hoping that I might get along with Baptiste. Your son is a fine gentleman indeed."

Claudine gently broke away from her. "It is I who must apologize. I bear a great responsibility in all of this. Everything I have done, I did in order to bring you and Guy together."

"What?"

Her friend bit her lip. "Don't get me wrong, Baptiste is a dear boy and I hold him in my heart as only a mother can, but he is not the man for you. I was hoping his presence might spur Guy into claiming your affections for himself. It worked all too well, I'm afraid. I had not counted on Victoire making such a mess of things.”

Antonia shook her head. She couldn’t blame Claudine for what she’d done with the best intentions at heart. After all, she was the one who had decided to trust Guy, and he was the one who had deceived her.

“It’s not Victoire’s fault. Nor is it yours. Guy might have claimed my affections, but he has none to give back.”

“My dear,” Claudine replied gently, “that is not true. It is immediately obvious to anyone with eyes that you are in love with each other.”

No. No, she couldn’t let herself believe it. If she gave in to the slightest hope… “You’re wrong. If he were truly in love with me—”

“He would ask you to marry him? It is not so simple, unfortunately. Sometimes love is not enough, and heartbreak is inevitable.”

She looked up at Claudine. Though her expression hadn’t changed, the cheerful sparkle in her eyes had given way to unmistakable sadness. Sadness that told Antonia all she needed to know without asking for details.

“Oh. I see.”

“Yes. It was very long ago. More than twenty years.”

“Does it get easier with time?”

“Some wounds never quite heal,” Claudine sighed, “but you build a life around them nonetheless. Monsieur Rouget was much older than I was when we married. I spent a year crying every night, thinking I would die from the anguish of being parted from the man I truly loved. But I learned to find happiness elsewhere. My husband was a good man and a good father, and our children brought us much joy.”

Marriage. Children. Joy. She couldn’t possibly imagine any of it, not now. But Claudine wouldn’t lie to her. “Do you regret any of it?”

“Regret is the most useless of all sentiments. But I will tell you this: if there had been the slightest chance for my beloved and I to be happy together, I would have seized it, and never looked back."

Antonia filed her words away in her mind. She would have several hours to mull them over on the way to Chartres.

"Thank you, Claudine," she said, and they embraced again. "For everything."

"It was my pleasure, believe me," Claudine replied, a glint of merriment returning to her gaze. "I didn't expect to have quite so much excitement during this stay."

THE STREETS OF Paris were dusty in the hot, dry air of July, and though the 14th had passed, many windows were still bedecked in blue, white and red ornaments. The whole city had been swept up in a frenzy of celebrations, and there had been balls, parades, fireworks.

Guy felt as if he was a spectator watching a play unfold on a stage, looking on passively from a distance, unable to fully understand what was happening, unwilling to make any effort to try.

He glanced around at the bustling crowd. Which street was this? Two women dressed in gauzy, almost transparent dresses, with loose curls falling from their bonnets and brightly colored shawls tucked into the crook of their bare arms, eyed him as he passed and giggled. He barely spared them a glance. The pleasures on display on every street corner and in every *salon* only managed to muster a faint impression of disgust in the pit of his belly. Like drinking still, tepid water after tasting the freshness of a mountain spring.

None of that now. Otherwise, he'd get lost again.

Finally, he spotted a street sign. Ah, yes, it was this way. Well, that was more than he'd been able to say a few weeks earlier, when he'd found himself wandering aimlessly in the city, putting one foot in front of the other simply to do something. It was either that or stay in his room and drink himself into oblivion.

Not that he wasn't tempted by that particular course of action when evening came and there was nothing to keep his thoughts at bay. However, at present, someone was waiting for him.

"Good morning, Monsieur de Cazal," the stable hand told him as he entered, suddenly enveloped by the smell of fresh hay and polished leather. "Would you like me to saddle Zephyr?"

"Thank you, but I'd rather do it myself."

The stable hand nodded politely. "As you wish, *monsieur*."

He'd been surprised the first few times Guy had answered him in a similar manner; Guy supposed not many gentlemen who left their horses at the stables bothered to groom and saddle them.

He walked down the row of stalls—all spacious and clean, he'd made sure of that when he'd visited the establishment. When he arrived at the end, two sharp, black eyes stared at him through the dimness, and the horse stretched his neck, pressing his muzzle into Guy's palm.

"Eager for a ride, are you?" Guy said with a half-smile. "I can understand the need to stretch one's legs, believe me."

Zephyr whickered, and Guy patted his neck. He still couldn't quite believe the horse was his—*his*, not just on loan. François had written to him two weeks earlier, renewing his offer to sell him Zephyr, as well as a host of other proposals for his consideration. For Guy, the choice had been a simple one: purchase Zephyr or burn the letter and forget he'd ever been to Verneuil. Either way, he couldn't bear thinking too long about it.

Why hadn't he chosen the second option? Why burden himself with Zephyr's upkeep, when he could barely take care of himself? The reason eluded him even now.

But when he finally put his feet in the stirrups, settled in the saddle and set off for the Champs Élysées, he was once again reminded of why he spent so much time riding, when nothing else elicited the slightest interest in him. At a slow canter, under the leafy shade of the trees, riding Zephyr gave him a similar sensation as the one he'd had in Verneuil, the thrill of freedom and possibility.

The heat of summer and the smell of fresh grass. And her. Her eyes, her lips, her body, her soft, low voice.

None of that. He needed to clear his head.

On and on and on he rode, until his horse was winded and his flanks were drenched in sweat, and his own thighs were burning from exertion. The illusion always had to end sooner or later.

Guy took off his hat and wiped his brow with his handkerchief. A few meters away from him, a gentleman and a lady were riding their mounts at a slow pace while they conversed in low voices.

His stomach plummeted. He tried to keep the image at bay but it reeled through his mind with the force of a gale.

Antonia riding beside him. Antonia seated atop a gentle, even-tempered mare he would have selected himself with the greatest care. Nothing would be too good for her. He would guide her, show her how to master her horse, and they would ride together in the country, and every hill and road and landscape would be renewed in beauty and wonder from her presence.

His throat clenched. *Antonia.* He had broken her heart. Shattered her innocence. And he was all too aware that these things could not be repaired.

He tugged on the reins and headed back toward the city. He couldn't dwell, or it would break him as well.

By the time he'd taken Zephyr back to the stables and groomed him, it was well past noon, and the afternoon stretched before him with agonizing emptiness. He headed at a brisk pace toward Palais Royal.

The palace itself, once the majestic residence of the king's brother, was a labyrinth of galleries and arcades housing shops of every kind and sins for every taste. Guy walked along the northern gallery, busy with vendors and customers, then turned into a narrow, winding alleyway littered with refuse. A few minutes later, he arrived at a small, dilapidated church. Saint Aphrodise had been sacked during the Revolution and had stayed abandoned ever since.

He entered the empty nave through the side door. Shouts echoed off the walls, coming from two men fighting in a makeshift ring. Nicolas followed the action, calling out directions. He spotted Guy and gave him a nod, but waited until the match was done to greet him.

"Come straight after riding again?" he said with a glance at his outfit. "Did you stop for luncheon at least?"

"Not hungry," Guy grunted, taking off his jacket. Hopefully one of the two combatants was ready for another round.

"When's the last time you ate?"

Guy shrugged. He was content with a piece of bread and a slice of cheese here and there, but anything more substantial turned to dust on his palate.

Nicolas shook his head and crossed his arms over his chest. "That's a shame. I'm not keen on fighting a half-starved opponent. No glory in winning."

"What do you mean?"

He took off his shirt and stretched his arms. "Get in here, de Cazal. I'll be your sparring partner today."

If that was how he wanted it, fine. Guy didn't have anything to lose at this point. At least he wouldn't have an audience: one nod toward the door was all it had taken for the two other men to follow Nicolas's order and leave.

Guy stripped off his boots, stockings and shirt and climbed over the ropes, raising his fisted hands. Ready. Familiarity told him Nicolas's reflexes were lightning fast. Nicolas edged toward him, bouncing on the balls of his feet. Bobbing. Offering almost nothing as a target. Still, Guy lashed out with a fist. Not fast enough. Worse, he left an opening. In a swift whirling motion, Nicolas's foot whipped up and caught him square in the jaw. Pain blinded him, and he crashed to the floor, wincing on impact.

Devil take it. The bastard wasn't holding back this time.

"Had enough?" Nicolas panted.

Guy got up again and spat, leaving a crimson blotch on the smooth stone. "I don't know what you're trying to prove but…"

"I'm not trying to prove anything," Nicolas replied, almost calmly. "I'm trying to beat you into submission. Then maybe you'll listen to me."

The moment Guy scrambled to his feet, Nicholas rained a series of relentless blows on him. A fist to the chest, another to the gut, a foot to the kidneys. Damnation, he'd never known such sharp pain. He could barely avoid the pummeling let alone mount any sort of attack. Nicolas could maim him if he chose to. Kill him even. He was perfectly in control of the amount of hurt he was inflicting, just enough to inexorably wear him down.

Finally, Guy held up his hands in forfeit, then slumped against the ropes, his heart pounding and his lungs screaming for air. Nicolas took a few moments to catch his own breath, then turned back to him.

"Right. Down to business, then. How long are you going to keep this up?"

"Keep what up?"

He knew. Of course, he knew. But after the beating he'd just taken, he wasn't about to let Nicolas needle him so easily.

"Exhausting yourself while barely eating, and God only knows if you're sleeping more than a few hours a night. You take better care of that damn horse."

Guy gave a joyless laugh. "Would you rather I gamble and whore my nights away like I did when we met?"

Nicolas ducked between the ropes to pat himself down with a cloth, then put his shirt back on. "Funny thing you should mention that. I never did tell you why I saved your life that night."

Guy waited for him to continue, still slumped against the wall, avoiding his friend's gaze but listening intently.

"True, on the surface there was nothing to distinguish you

from the poor devils wasting away in gaming hells. You were just as desperate and pathetic as the rest of them."

"Is that supposed to make me feel better?"

"Would you rather I talked, or do you want to go another round with me? The reason you stood out is because you weren't numb, desensitized by your misfortune. It was plain to see you were angry and grieving, and that all the decadent behavior in Palais Royal wasn't enough to blunt your emotions."

"Well," Guy snorted, "perhaps I was just going the wrong way about it."

"No. You can channel your feelings, and that's why I taught you how to fight. You can sweep them under the rug for a little while in order to indulge in more pleasant pursuits. But you can't make them disappear entirely. What happened with Antonia was inevitable."

Guy looked up sharply. It was the first time Nicolas had pronounced her name in front of him since they'd returned from Verneuil.

"You don't know what you're talking about."

Nicolas raised an eyebrow. "Don't I? Forgive me, but I know what it's like to have one's father lose his head to the Widow."

A father, and a brother. And Nicolas had witnessed the executions. In fact, that was one of the reasons they'd implicitly trusted each other after that first evening. Guy didn't have to hide anything from Nicolas, and he didn't have to explain why he was staying in Paris, living a life of indolence with no concern for what would happen tomorrow.

Until now.

"It's time to stop hiding, man," Nicolas continued. "You're not a banker like your father, and you never will be. But you're not a jaded bourgeois or a hardened street fighter either, and least of all a *débauché*. I will always be your loyal friend and ally, but Paris is not the place for you."

Antonia's words echoed through his mind. *A débauché doesn't care about anyone, or anything. You care.*

Guy stood up. His body seemed to be in working order again, though he'd be able to count the bruises on his body in a few hours. "Even if you were right, I wouldn't know where else to go."

"You do know. The question is if you'll have the bollocks to go back there." Nicolas tossed him a cloth. "If nothing else, it'll be a nice change of scenery for your horse after galloping up and down the Champs Élysées every bloody morning."

Chapter Fifteen

"LOOK, I'VE FINISHED. She's very pretty, isn't she?"

Antonia turned away from the window of the drawing room to Jeanne, who was holding out her doll. The jointed toy was wearing a small dress of red brocade, the same cloth that Honorine had recently used to make new cushion covers. The doll, a vacant gaze and a fixed smile painted on her porcelain face, started back at Antonia.

Which was about the same as Antonia herself had felt for days. Weeks. How long had it been? Time had blurred into an endless stretch of misery. At least she had stopped crying every night.

"Very pretty indeed," she told Jeanne. "Your sewing skills are improving. Did you design her dress yourself?"

"Yes, I copied it from a print that *Maman* got at the haberdashery. It says it's the latest fashion in Paris." The little girl's eyes shone with excitement. "You saw ladies from Paris, didn't you? Are they all beautiful and elegant?"

"I suppose so, yes."

She didn't want to add that the most beautiful and elegant of them all had also been ill-mannered and cruel. The only small satisfaction she had experienced lately was when Claudine had written in her last letter than Xavier de Brienne was now engaged to be married, and that Victoire's lack of funds had forced her to return to her own husband, who had henceforth refused to fund her Parisian lifestyle.

"Hush, now, leave your aunt alone," Honorine intervened. "I need your help polishing the silverware."

Jeanne gave a groan. "But I wanted to start working on her slippers!"

"That's all right, I'll help you," Antonia said.

"Are you certain, dear?"

Antonia nodded. The worst of her anguish came when she had nothing to keep her hands busy or her mind occupied. If Honorine had an unlimited supply of silver to polish or handkerchiefs to embroider, she would do it and gladly.

Every day was the same: trying to find one occupation after another, from daybreak to nightfall. She couldn't read with her mind drifting back to Guy. Couldn't take a walk in the countryside without imagining his handsome figure atop a horse, riding on the horizon. Couldn't even lie in her bed at night without remembering the weight of him on top of her, his sure hands and his eager mouth, his deep blue eyes setting her skin aflame when he looked at her as no one else ever had.

She didn't want to remember any of it. Yet she was terrified of forgetting. How long would it take until Guy faded from her mind and her heart? Perhaps the pain would lessen, but it was all she had left.

For she had no hope of seeing Guy again. Not since Stanislas had announced at dinner, with an unusual amount of precaution, that Lazare Fournier was the new owner of the De Cazal bank. Word about town was that he had acquired it at a ridiculously low price, which everyone thought was fair given the amount of work he'd put in to get it running again.

Antonia knew what that meant. Guy was never coming back. The last little spark that still palpitated within her had been snuffed out, leaving only a splintered heart.

She followed her sister to the dining room and they settled at the table with two strips of chamois and boxes of silverware. But polishing the forks failed to lull her mind or numb her senses. Instead, a frantic, overwhelming urge started to build up within her.

What if she ran away to Paris? What if she found him, and told him she wanted to stay with him, regardless of her status or what anyone said?

Absurd. She wouldn't even know where to look, adrift in a sea of strangers. Here she was safe, wanting for nothing, surrounded by people who truly loved and valued her.

But damn him, she simply couldn't settle for that any longer. Guy had robbed her of her capacity to find contentment in familiarity and routine. Or perhaps she had never been that content to begin with, and he'd only torn away the veil she had let settle on her life.

Either way, she was trapped.

She let the fork drop on the table, blinked away hot tears.

"Antonia," Honorine said, and reached for her hand. "What is the matter, dear? You're not… in a delicate situation, are you?"

Her sister, bless her, had never asked for details regarding her stay at Verneuil, though Antonia supposed Lisette had told her everything she needed to know. On that particular matter, however, the maid had apparently been discreet.

"No, no, I… I had my courses last week."

Honorine let out a little breath. "Ah. That's a relief. What is it, then?"

"Nothing," Antonia murmured, shaking her head. "I… I…"

A flurry of excited squeals interrupted her. Momentarily distracted, Antonia rushed with Honorine to the drawing room to find the children gathered at the windows, waving at someone in the courtyard.

Antonia looked over Jeanne's head. The groom had opened the carriage door to let a cart through, and the groundskeeper was unloading a hefty trunk from the back with the help of another man.

Tall and sturdy, with light brown hair and a short beard of the same coloring over his square jaw, he strained to set the trunk on the ground, then looked up at the window. There were dark circles under his gray eyes.

"Jerome," Honorine said in a strangled tone. "Thank the heavens, our brother has returned. We are all together now."

Antonia covered her mouth, and the tears finally found their way down her cheeks.

HOME.

The word echoed in Jerome's mind as he took in his surroundings. The large bay windows overlooking the garden in the summer twilight. The large oak table covered with a white tablecloth, where he sat between his two sisters before a hearty dinner. The three eldest children now sat with the rest of the family, while their siblings played in the background under the watchful eye of their grandparents, who smiled upon them from a large painting on the wall.

Home. He hadn't been here in so long, it was like a waking dream. He wanted to bask in the feeling, settle in it like in a warm bath after a long journey, but something was keeping him from doing so.

Antonia, for one. Eyes downcast, face drawn, though she had greeted him with an effusion of emotion that wasn't unusual for her. It had not been a year since she had left London with Honorine, Stanislas and the children to return to Chartres, while Jerome had stayed behind to finish his apprenticeship. But even in that short period of time, she had changed. She was more somber, held herself differently, stood straighter, shoulders back. And when she lifted her eyes, they were filled with a depth he didn't remember seeing before. All trace of awkwardness or shyness had melted away, but so had her innocent, artless good humor. Had he been there to protect her…

You must return in all haste, Honorine had written to him a few weeks before. *There are certain things for which Stanislas cannot replace you as head of our family, particularly when it comes to the well-being of our dear sister. Antonia, I fear, is facing certain difficulties…*

She had not expounded on the nature of these difficulties, but it made no difference. He had stayed far too long in London. He had let his personal interest for his apprenticeship and his desire for freedom supplant his sense of duty.

You are free to do what you please, are you not? At least for one night…

He chased away the echoes in his head. No. He must stifle that memory, forget it ever happened. He reached for his wine glass and took a long, slow drink, then turned to Stanislas.

"Business has been good, then? I'm pleased to hear it."

Stanislas grunted. He was a man of few words, but they had never needed many to understand each other. "Lots of rebuilding to do still."

"You've handled it well. Secured the trust of our artisans and workers. Small wonder the orders keep rolling in."

Honorine dabbed her mouth with her napkin. "Perhaps you could find work as an architect's assistant in Paris, once you've spent some time with us. I hear there are great renovations planned for the capital."

"We'll see." Jerome glanced at Antonia, who still hadn't spoken a word. "I've only just returned. Now I wish to focus on my family's happiness."

Under his insistent gaze, Antonia finally lifted her head and the ghost of a smile passed over her lips. "Well, I am happy you're here, brother."

He forced a smile in return, but his mind was reeling with the need for more information. And damn if Honorine wasn't going to tell him everything she knew.

Once dinner was over and the children were in bed, they settled in the well-worn chairs of the drawing room. Honorine was repairing one of the girls' skirts, while Stanislas quietly smoked a pipe, deep in thought. Antonia had an open book in her hands, as usual, but her eyes weren't focused on the page. They were lost somewhere.

Or lost because of someone. After all, the reasons for that sort of melancholy were few, and one was sadly more frequent than any other. His hands curled into fists on his thighs.

"What is it you're reading there, Toinette?"

She snapped her book shut, as if he'd startled her. "Chateaubriand. But I fear my attention is dwindling." She rose from the divan. "I bid all of you good night."

"Good night, Antonia," Honorine replied, and met Jerome's eye over her sewing.

"Will you tell me what the devil is going on?" he finally hissed once Antonia had left the room.

Honorine let the skirt fall to her knees. "Fine." She laid a gentle hand on Stanislas's shoulder. "My love, will you allow us some privacy? You've heard all of this already."

Stanislas nodded, put out his pipe and kissed Honorine's hand before retiring.

"Go on, then," Jerome said. "Though you might have saved us some time and explained what happened in the letter you sent me."

She gave a little laugh. "Ha! So you could work yourself up in a murderous rage for a week before getting here? A load of good that would have done you."

Murderous. There was only one thing that could possibly push him to take out his pistol and serve justice: if anyone harmed a member of his family. And it wasn't hard to guess the type of harm Antonia had run into.

"Now I feel like I don't need details," he growled. "Just a name. Who is he?"

Honorine paused before answering. "Guy de Cazal."

The name momentarily stunned him out of his anger. "Joseph and Marguerite's son? The one our parents wanted Toinette to marry all those years ago?"

"The very same. They met again recently, at a house party, and… well, Antonia didn't say anything, but Lisette informed me that they… renewed their acquaintance."

The anger returned, dark and rumbling like a storm. He struggled to keep his voice even. "Am I to understand that this bounder dishonored my sister and has gone unpunished for it?"

Honorine gave him a stern look that was eerily similar to their mother's. "Now, Jerome, before you go galloping off on your horse in the dead of night with a loaded pistol, listen to me. Lisette has assured me, in no uncertain terms, that whatever happened between them was mutually agreed upon."

"Good God, what a load of drivel," he boomed, and stood from his chair to pace across the room. "Toinette is a delicate, innocent young woman. Or at least she *was*. She cannot agree to that sort of thing."

"*Antonia* is twenty-four, and entirely capable of making her own decisions in matters of the heart," Honorine countered.

"*Matters of the heart*? That's a very gracious way of putting it."

"Yet it is true. You should be less concerned with dishonor, and more concerned with her heartbreak and distress. If I told you to come back, it's because I was worried about her, not because I needed a champion for her virtue."

He stopped in front of the window and stared into the blue darkness beyond. "It doesn't matter. If he seduced her without offering for her, he must face the consequences."

She heaved a great sigh. "Oh, Jerome. You have always upheld such high standards for yourself, you have not the slightest understanding for anyone who falls short of them."

Take what you want. Take me.

He closed his eyes for a moment, struggled to push back the image of silky black hair and creamy skin. One night of folly before leaving London. One night where he had left reason and honor at the doorstep of a room decked in red velvet.

Tell me what it is you most desire. Your secrets will be safe with me.

It wouldn't happen again. But he couldn't deny he himself had failed before.

"Very well," he relented. "I won't go looking for him. But if our paths ever cross, mark my words, he will pay."

Chapter Sixteen

GUY URGED ZEPHYR through the gates of Lazare Fournier's house and into the busy street. Chartres was the same as he remembered it, tall houses of gray stone sitting serenely in the shadow of the cathedral along the Eure river.

He'd returned and pulled through. He'd met with Fournier and their business had gone well. The man had been polite, compassionate even. He hadn't worded a single reproach for Guy's months of silence. No doubt the bank would be in good hands with Fournier at the helm. The man had even offered to oversee the sale of the De Cazal estate, though it had fallen into grave disrepair over the past ten years.

Ransacked, probably, and overrun with weeds. Guy didn't want to see it. If there was one last memory he wanted to keep intact, it was his mother's rose garden, blooming with re-splendent color in the spring sunshine. And he needed all the courage he could muster for a far more important task.

Heart thumping hard against his chest, he turned his mount onto a paved road leading away from the city and into a verdant hamlet.

He stopped in front of a large, sturdy country house whose outer wall was overgrown with ivy. Hands trembling, he dismounted Zephyr and kept his reins in hand while he rang the bell. The *porte cochère* opened and a young groom appeared, eyes wide and questioning.

"Guy de Cazal," he introduced himself. "I wish to speak to…"

He hesitated. It was not proper to ask for Antonia directly. He should at least speak to her brother-in-law first. The vague memories he had of Stanislas and the few things Antonia had mentioned painted him as a quiet, reserved man, but Guy would gladly face whatever drubbing was in store for him.

The young groom gawked at him.

"I wish to speak to the master of the house," he finished.

The groom nodded and took Zephyr's reins from him. Guy stood for a few minutes by the door, taking in his surroundings. The old stone well in the corner of the courtyard, the potted flowers at the window of the gatekeeper's cottage, the chickens ambling around freely—just as he remembered. But for one essential, insurmountable difference, he could very well have found himself ten years into the past.

A sudden shout shattered his thoughts.

"—in the courtyard? How dare he even cross the threshold of this house?"

Not a shout. A roar.

"Jerome, please!" a feminine voice cried. "Contain yourself!"

Jerome. A cold sweat ran down Guy's back. Oh no. This wasn't good. This wasn't good *at all.*

"To hell with containing myself! I'll kill him if I bloody well please!"

Antonia's brother appeared in Guy's line of sight. Jerome Saint Yves was a head taller than he was, with a hulking frame that brought to mind a stonemason rather than an architect.

Guy squared his shoulders. Getting to Antonia would certainly be more arduous than he expected, but he wasn't going to back down, and he could at least defend himself with sufficient skill. Attacking Jerome, though… That was little more than a death wish.

"*You,*" Jerome bellowed, his face contorted in rage. "I ought to gut you where you stand!"

"Saint Yves," Guy replied. "If you would just let me—"

Jerome grabbed him brusquely by the collar with both hands. "What? Explain? You *bastard*. There is nothing to explain. I know everything."

Guy grabbed his wrists, trying to push him back. Good God, the man had muscles like granite. "And I deny nothing. I have come to make amends."

"Very well. If you truly wish to make amends, I will not pound your face into a pulp, and we will settle this tomorrow at dawn."

"Jerome! Let him go!"

Another voice. *Hers*. Guy glanced over Jerome's shoulder. Antonia was standing next to her sister a few meters away, shock etched on her face. So beautiful, even now. His starving eyes took her in avidly.

Jerome's grip didn't loosen. "You know the rules, sister. He knows them too."

"I do not wish to duel with you," Guy said.

"You should have thought of that before compromising my sister and refusing to marry her."

"You're right. It was a grave error, and I sincerely wish to rectify it."

Jerome looked at him intently for a few seconds. "If you think for a moment I would let you marry Antonia…"

Guy swallowed. He might get beaten to a pulp yet, but he had to speak his heart. "It is not your permission I seek, but her acceptance."

He heard her take in a breath. Now she knew. But would she hear him out? Though he needed to breach this particular wall first, it was nothing compared to the task that lay ahead. But Antonia deserved no less than a battle.

IT WAS ALL happening too fast. Too suddenly. One moment, she and Honorine had been playing with the children in the drawing room, and the next…

Guy. Here, in the courtyard. His blue eyes blazing, his jaw clenched with determination, standing up to Jerome, who was gripping him by the collar as if he meant to throw him against the wall.

Jerome *knew*.

"By God, Honorine, why did you tell him?" she cried.

"What choice did I have?" Honorine replied helplessly. "I was worried for you, and I couldn't lie to him. I never thought Guy would show up at our door!"

Neither had Antonia. Not even in the waking dreams that sometimes slipped past her resignation.

And yet this was no dream. This was reality, another absurd twist of fate descending upon her without warning.

"It is not your permission I seek, but her acceptance."

She forgot to breathe for a moment. She must have heard wrong. He could not possibly mean…

"Without my permission, you will not get within three meters of her," Jerome growled.

Honorine threw her hands in the air and let them fall back on her thighs. "Brother, for goodness' sake, let the man state his case."

Jerome finally let go of Guy's collar. "Fine. You have five minutes. And you'll both stay where I can see you."

"No," Antonia stated, stepping forward. If she was to hear what Guy had to say, it would certainly not be in front of her brother. "I will not have you watch me like Honorine does the children. Believe me, I will protest loudly and vigorously if anything untoward happens."

Guy looked at her, and their gazes met.

Still so deep, so intense. Aching for her. But not with hunger, as it had before. With desperation.

Her heart swelled, longing for him, longing to mend, to beat without hurting. A storm of doubt and resentment raged in her mind. Jerome was right. How dare he show up here without a word of notice, after weeks of silence?

She crossed her arms in front of her chest, turning away to go sit on the stone bench near the well.

"If my sister so much as raises her voice, de Cazal," Jerome said, "my pistol will be loaded and ready to send you to meet your maker. Understood?"

"Understood."

Her siblings returned inside the house. Suddenly, the court-yard was empty but for the two of them. Guy slowly approached, standing next to the bench, his hands clasped behind his back.

"It seems absurd to ask you how you've been," he murmured.

"Yes, let us forgo any semblance of politeness," she retorted. "After all, you came to my home without bothering to send me a letter and ask if I would receive you."

"I didn't want to hide behind a piece of paper. I thought you deserved to hear what I had to say, or else tell me to burn in the fires of hell, in person."

She bit her lower lip. Both options appealed equally to her. "Speak, then. Your time is running out."

Guy gave a short nod. "After I returned to Paris, François wrote to me. He thought I might be interested in purchasing Zephyr—his horse. Well, *my* horse now. The one I rode when we were in Verneuil."

She frowned. What did this have to do with her?

"He also had a proposition for me," he continued. "He's been wanting to start a business to breed, train and sell horses for a few years now, but he could never find the right partner. Now he has."

Antonia's mouth opened in surprise. "You're going to work with François Aubertin?"

"I sold the bank to Lazare Fournier and reinvested my fa-ther's assets. I'm also looking to buy property not far from

Verneuil."

The bank. That was why he'd handed it over. Not because he never planned on returning. But then... She looked up at him. "Why are you telling me this?"

He smoothed his coat, fiddled with his cuffs. Trying to figure out what to do with his hands, a nervous habit of his. Oh, how she wished she could take them in hers. Feel them on her skin again. But no. She couldn't simply fall into his arms again and trust him to catch her. She would not survive having her heart broken twice.

"I'm trying to figure out the man I want to be," he replied. "Not the man my father wanted me to be, to be sure. But someone with a purpose in life. And I... I can't be that man if you're not by my side, Antonia."

Her pulse quickened with dizzying speed, and she gripped the edge of the stone bench for balance. "And what of the woman I want to be? Do you think I can become *anything* if I keep forgetting myself for the benefit of others?"

"No, that's not what I—"

She rose to her feet, a turmoil of emotions sweeping through her. "I am done trying to please everyone around me. When we were in Verneuil... You taught me how to ask for what I want. How to free myself from people's opinions. How to be bold. And seeing you now makes it all the clearer that I cannot go back."

He drew in a sharp breath, but said nothing, waiting for her to go on.

"What you said that night, about there being no honor in settling down, in love, in marriage..." She could hardly bear remembering his words. The words that had driven through her heart like a knife. Now it was her turn to wield them. "*That* is what I want. And I cannot risk my only chance at happiness with someone who might hurt me again."

"I was wrong," he said in a quiet voice. "So very wrong..."

"Those are just words, Guy," she countered furiously. "Words mean *nothing*. What could possibly make you change in so little time?"

He looked at her with steady resolve. "I told you I didn't want to die for love like my mother. But it's too late now. I love you too much. There is no true life I can imagine living without you."

Words meant nothing. All words, except those. An echo of her own feelings, rising to the surface, overwhelming her, impossible to contain or to deny.

He stepped closer to her and took her hand with trembling fingers.

"I can't..." she whispered.

"Please, Antonia," he rasped. "Please. I will wait, however long you need me to. A month. A year. Ten more years, if that's what it takes, only..."

"No, I meant..." She shook her head. "I can't stand being parted from you. God knows I have tried to reason with myself, but I am in agony when we are apart."

His hand tightened around hers. "We don't have to be. Ever again. No matter if the world around us falls apart once more."

She nodded, and he pulled her into his warm embrace, kissing her hair, her temple, her lips. Glorious relief shone through. *Heaven.* She had never known the meaning of the word before.

"My beautiful, beloved Antonia." He kissed her again, and again. "Say you'll marry me. Say you'll be my wife."

"Yes. *Yes.*" She smiled up at him. "I will."

He grinned and pressed his forehead against hers. "Now that you have accepted me, shall I ask your brother for his approval? Or should I wait a few days until he calms down?"

Antonia laughed. "Let me speak to him first. I should be able to make him unhand his pistol within the hour."

He raised an eyebrow. "In a hurry, are you?"

She laid one more kiss on his lips. "If I have anything to say about it, it'll be a very short betrothal indeed."

Epilogue

Domaine d'Orgeval, November 1801

A COLD WIND swept russet leaves across the beaten dirt of the stable yard, and gray clouds rolled overhead. Guy looked at the path that led to the gates of the estate and beyond. No rain on the horizon. The perfect weather for a ride in the countryside.

Antonia sauntered across the stable yard. "Is Atlas saddled yet, my darling?"

Though he had seen her not an hour before at breakfast, his gaze still lingered over every last detail of her figure. Her dark blue wool riding coat hugged her shapely figure. The high collar and matching hat were lined with gray fur. At first, she'd protested at the extra expense. A riding outfit was an extravagance on top of her wedding gown and the new day dresses that befitted her new status as mistress of her own home. But Guy had stifled her protests with kisses until she was too breathless to complain. He was proud to lavish her with gifts. What good was regaining his family's fortune if he could not spend it on worthwhile pursuits?

And pleasing his wife was his best investment, for the return was hundredfold.

"The horses will be ready in a moment," he replied, reaching for her hand and pulling her closer. "You look simply ravishing."

She smiled and adjusted his cravat, her fingers fiddling with the edges. "Silly, this is the same coat I've worn for every other riding lesson. There's mud on the hem and Lord knows what else."

"That takes nothing away from your beauty." He tilted her chin up for a kiss. "Especially when you are riding by my side."

Antonia sighed. "Poor Zephyr. I can't imagine how tedious it must be for him to go at the same pace as Atlas."

Atlas was an old gelding who, when pushed, might break out into a lazy trot for a few minutes before returning to a plod—the precise reason why Guy had acquired him. A placid, harmless mount would reassure Antonia while she learned.

But today, he had a different plan.

The clopping of hooves resounded through the yard. They both turned. A stable hand led Zephyr, flanked by a smaller chestnut.

Antonia emitted a sharp gasp. "Guy, what is… Whose horse is this?"

He smiled and took the reins of the mare. Her coat was glossy as copper, her limbs fine and well-proportioned, her gait graceful and measured. He had ridden her himself a few times before purchasing her so nothing would be left to chance, and she obeyed his slightest command.

Soft, even-tempered, but capable of a fast gallop once you let her have her head. The perfect match for Antonia.

"She is yours, my love," he said, handing her the reins. "Her name is Satine."

She took them with a trembling hand, her eyes widening. "Oh, she is a beauty. Guy…" She took a shaky breath. "You shouldn't have. It is too much."

"You did not expect to ride poor old Atlas forever, did you? I think it's time to put him to pasture. He's earned his retirement."

Her expression dimmed, and she frowned. Every once in a while, traces of her old insecurities rose to the surface, especially since they had moved to Orgeval. Though she was not shy in indulging in the many pleasures of married life, managing her own household staff was new to her, and learning to ride had also been a challenge.

"I am not certain I can ride such a horse, lovely though she may be," she murmured. "If I pull the reins too hard... Or if she decides she doesn't want me on her back..."

"Horses are intelligent animals. More perceptive, in many ways, than men."

A teasing smile returned to her lips. "Humans, you mean, or just men? If it's the latter I'm fully willing to believe it."

He grinned and tucked a loose curl behind her ear. "If you want to be on her back, she will sense it. If you treat her with a firm but kind hand, she will respect you. I have no doubt the two of you will get along marvelously."

Antonia stroked the mare's neck. "Well, she certainly is a most refined lady."

"Trust me, I have been searching far and wide for such a specimen since our engagement."

She turned back to him, her cheeks rosy, her eyes shining. A bright, loving gaze she reserved for him, and him alone. His heart quivered. Had he thought the return was a hundredfold? He was wrong. It was in the thousands.

"I trust you." She stepped onto the mounting block and grabbed one of the horns of the side-saddle. "Always."

He swung his leg over Zephyr's back and settled into his seat, and they headed toward the gates at a leisurely walk. No need to rush. They had all the time in the world, and just being at Antonia's side gave him more contentment than he'd ever known.

"How are you finding her?" he asked.

Antonia leaned forward to pat Satine's neck. "Splendid. It's like riding a cloud. Shall we go a bit faster?"

He raised an eyebrow. "Ready for a trot, then?"

Antonia nodded eagerly. Ah, there it was. The passion that

lay hidden under her reserve. A century could pass, and he would never tire of coaxing it out of her.

"I think I am, yes. After all, soon I will have to learn how to gallop to keep up with you."

He turned Zephyr so he was close to grasp her gloved hand and kiss it. "As you well know, my love, I most enjoy being your teacher."

THE END

ABOUT THE AUTHOR

Twenty years after studying history at the Sorbonne, Delphine Roy put her classwork to good use in her spicy historical romances set in Post-Revolutionary France. Before that, she spent a good part of her childhood on both sides of the Atlantic and started writing stories in French and English. Her teenage self may have posted them in online fanfiction forums that thankfully no longer exist.

Delphine now lives in the suburbs of Paris with her husband and her son. She's a high school ESL teacher by day and an author by night of romance (in English) and fantasy (in French). In her free time, she enjoys cross-stitching, watching hockey and going down Wikipedia wormholes.